WIDE LOOP

Center Point
Large Print

Also by Nelson Nye and available from
Center Point Large Print:

The Killer of Cibecue

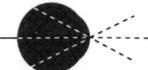

**This Large Print Book carries the
Seal of Approval of N.A.V.H.**

WIDE LOOP

Nelson Nye

CENTER POINT LARGE PRINT
THORNDIKE, MAINE

WESTERN
NYE

This Center Point Large Print edition
is published in the year 2018 by arrangement with
Golden West Literary Agency.

First US edition: Dodd, Mead & Company
First UK edition: Ward Lock

The text of this Large Print edition is unabridged.
In other aspects, this book may vary
from the original edition.
Printed in the United States of America
on permanent paper.
Set in 16-point Times New Roman type.

ISBN: 978-1-68324-829-3 (hardcover)
ISBN: 978-1-68324-833-0 (paperback)

Library of Congress Cataloging-in-Publication Data

Names: Nye, Nelson C. (Nelson Coral), 1907-1997, author.
Title: Wide loop / Nelson Nye.
Description: Center Point Large Print edition. | Thorndike, Maine :
    Center Point Large Print, 2018.
Identifiers: LCCN 2018009675| ISBN 9781683248293
    (hardcover : alk. paper) | ISBN 9781683248330 (pbk. : alk. paper)
Subjects: LCSH: Large type books. | GSAFD: Western stories.
Classification: LCC PS3527.Y33 W5 2018 | DDC 813/.54—dc23
LC record available at https://lccn.loc.gov/2018009675

For
RUTH
who helped build it

CONTENTS

ONE

"Go Get Him!"

Charlie Moore said angrily: "Deac makes the fifth in less than two months—that comes pretty damn near to being one stiff a week! This place is just made for the kinda game he's playin'. The boys can't fight phantoms. They can't ride fence and keep their eyes on the cattle. They can't do nothin' while they're all the time expecting to catch a slug between the ribs! You got seven hands left an' three of 'em right now is talkin' about quittin'."

"You know what will happen if he gets under this roof again! If I don't keep them riding—"

"Patrollin' the fence ain't going to keep him out. All that's done is left us wide open to every long rope on both sides of the line. I can't run this ranch without riders and we got a rep now as a bad spread to work for." He said impatiently, "If you wanta keep Dallas out, get Burt Alvord."

"That ignorant clown!"

The range boss peered at her slanchways and shrugged. "He's a card, all right; I ain't arguin' that part. Prob'ly eats with his knife an' uses bread for a pusher. Nothin' fancy about him. But he's got plenty of guts, which is a heap more

9

practical, an' when it comes to gunplay he can shave chain lightnin' with either hand."

"I don't want Dallas murdered."

"You want him kept off Bar 6. You ain't goin' to do it by snappin' a blanket. You got to use force or the threat of force, Bella. He ain't goin' to yell boo at no guy like Alvord."

She chewed at her lip. She drummed on the desk with her rope-scarred fingers. "Couldn't we find someone else?"

"What's the matter with Burt?"

"Oh—I don't know. I just don't like the sound of him—his rep. It's . . . it's *grubby*."

Charlie Moore snorted. "Anything you touch around here is grubby. You won't find no angels plowin' the dust of Tombstone. What you're needin's a man an' if you're aimin' to hang onto this place you better hire him."

"How about Wolf? Or Frank Aikens? Couldn't—"

"Wolf's off huntin' lobos. As for Aikens, you might as well compare Johnny Behan to Wyatt Earp. Besides, you couldn't trust him—"

"And what makes you think we could trust Burt Alvord?"

"Any man John Slaughter'd trust is good enough for me."

"I've heard—"

"Rumors!" Moore slammed the flat of a hand on his chair arm. "Now you listen to me!

10

Slaughter cleaned the crooks outa this county once an' Alvord was the lad he picked out to help him—an' Burt not even twenty at the time!" He stared at her grimly. "Hell's fire, girl, there's the man can get the job done!"

Bella Norton's blue-green glance poked quietly about the room which, up to five short months ago, had been her father's office. She was a well-made girl, lithe, full-breasted, with many of old Dave's mannerisms and much of his tenacity and vigor. He had built Bar 6 cow by cow and acre by acre into one of the sweetest outfits the border had ever seen, and his daughter was determined to keep it that way. She'd never known a mother's softness, had been raised with men and had a man's direct outlook, a man's way of going at things, discarding the chaff and cutting straight to fundamentals—which was largely the why of Moore's baffled irascibility. The issues here were plain, clean sliced. Was she about to go intuitive on him?

She wore puncher's garb and it took nothing from her; she had a figure that would catch and hold the eye of any man. She had a soft, appealing mouth in a face vaguely squared at the jaws and temples, large and penetrating eyes set beneath dark brows and dark gold curls framing cheeks as smooth as ivory. She was what Moore would call a *looker* and she had the brains to go with it. So why back and fill about this matter of hiring a gun fighter? You either beat Dallas off or he moved in and took over.

She said, still thinking about Alvord, "I've always rather imagined he was a pretty shiftless specimen."

"More easy goin' than shiftless. Just never had no partic'lar ambition—one of those guys that rolled in with the tumbleweeds. He come in on the gate of his ol' man's wagon when Tombstone was growin' the hair on its chest. Mother died a couple years later an' the Judge he took to soakin' up whisky. The kid spent most of his time round the sportin' crowd always mixed up in some kinda scrape at school—anything for a belly laugh. That's Burt, all right; you got that part straight.

"I remember," Moore said, "after Slaughter quit sheriffin', Burt got a job as day boss at the O. K. Corral where he'd learned some of the ruggeder aspects of life. Picked up with a young tough called Biddy Doyle . . ."

Biddy, it seemed, had been a whole lot of things at one time or another and got as big a bang from horseplay as Burt did. Dropped down to Bisbee bright and early one morning and set the word winging that he could out-box or out-wrestle any man alive. Lew Vidal got in touch and, acting as promoter, dug up a horny "Cousin Jack" who didn't mind "taking a crack at it." Biddy and Burt worked up some tall betting while

Burt tinkered around in the capacity of trainer.

Site of this match was to be a manure pile owned by Phelps-Dodge in Bisbee Canyon. The idea took hold, particularly with the sporting crowd; there were plenty who could see some very humorous possibilities in the vision of two other blokes rolling around in the turds. When the odds reached ten to one on the miner the man was bribed to throw the thing and Burt and his pals bet all they could borrow on Biddy.

It was quite a spectacle. After the match had been in progress some three or four minutes Biddy shoved his opponent's face in the muck and the miner, with a loud yell of being strangled, threw in the sponge. The crowd was stunned. But swiftly catching an odor of something that wasn't horse manure, they swarmed into the ring, angrily trying to get their hands on the culprits. Burt and Biddy barely managed to reach their waiting mounts. They hurried back to the O. K. Corral and divided their profits on Billy King's bar, though it cost Burt his job with Montgomery.

Another time he and Matt Berts went larking and, when they were ready to start for home, they wired the editor of the Tombstone *Epitaph*: Bodies of Berts and Alvord will arrive this afternoon.

The news spread like wildfire. You could hear any version you cared to listen to. They'd been in a gun fight. They'd tangled with Mexicans.

They'd got mixed up with some woman and her husband had caught them. The one thing all stories had in common was the assurance of fatality. A delegation was on hand to meet the stage when it pulled up before the O. K. Corral. Alvord and Berts swung down with big grins. " 'Course our bodies arrived," they guffawed— "we never go noplace without 'em."

But back of this predilection for pranks, Moore said, Burt Alvord had proved himself a man to ride the river with. John Slaughter, the cow boss pointed out, had always spoken highly of Burt. He had a lot of friends. He'd taken a job with Wells Fargo as shotgun messenger and never, while Burt's black-browed face was by the driver's, had they lost so much as one piece of bullion.

He'd been an undercover agent put to watching the border and had turned up more crooks than a man could shake a stick at.

When they'd struck gold at Pearce and things began to get ugly with the homicide rate making space in Eastern dailies, the camp fathers had remembered Burt Alvord—the man who never missed. They had asked him to come over and he had pinned on the star and, before a reasonably quick man could have said Jack Robinson, Pearce became "quiet as a cow pasture at midnight."

"You've heard what's been goin' on over at Willcox—how that damfool election got the tin hung onto that half-breed tamale-eater, an' how the cow crowd around there's been raisin' hell about it? Guy's brother-in-law runs a store an' all the rannies from the ranches has been helpin' theirselves, darin' this bean-lover to lift a hand ag'in' 'em. Last week they shot up three saloons, ransacked a hardware an' choused a team an' wagon through the side of the jail. What you prob'ly ain't heard is, the Board of Supervisors over there has sent Burt a invite. If you're wantin' him for Dallas you better get a move on."

He saw by the look of her face he'd overdone it. Growling under his breath he shoved out his saddle-bowed legs and, settling back in his chair, commenced shaping up a smoke. He was not at all surprised when she said with a trace of her father's dryness: "You working for Bar 6 or this gun fighter?"

Wrapping his jowls about the edge of a grin he rasped a match across a pantsleg, got his quirley going and snapped the stick into the fireplace. "Thanks for catchin' hold of the reins—guess the thought of that feller was about to run away with me. You're right; we don't want no hired guns on Bar 6. He prob'ly wouldn't take the job even if you was to offer it to him."

She asked with a sudden frown, "Why not?"

"Ridin' herd on a spoiled brat? He'd figure you was tryin' to get a laugh on him someway."

Moore, taking a drag on his hand-rolled, got up

with a creak of knee joints. He reached for his hat, Bella eyeing him suspiciously. She was a pretty smart trick for a kid of eighteen summers. "Where you off to?"

Charlie Moore had come into this country with Bella's father forty years ago, long before Tombstone had mushroomed on silver. He had known it in its wildest days. He hadn't come through all those birthings and buryings without picking up a certain amount of guile. "Goin' to see if I can't round up some more hands; haven't tried at Bonita or Hereford yet. Some of them spreads in the Aravaipa—"

"Any hands worth hiring have been hired by now."

"Sure they have," Charlie nodded, "but it's neck meat or nothin'. We're bein' stole blind an' you can't expect the boys to like these drygulchin's. They're layin' 'em to Dallas—"

"You know Dallas wouldn't—"

"Not personally, mebbe, but he's behind this business an' so long as you're content—"

"That's not fair to me, Charlie."

"Then, for Christ's sake, why don't you *do* somethin' about it? It wasn't *me* put the boys to patrollin' those fences. It wasn't *me* give them orders not to shoot back or—"

"Blood's thicker than water!"

"I ain't denyin' it. We all know you got a tough row to hoe. But what about the blood of them

16

five boys we've lost? That kid's turned wolf an' you got to turn with him or climb outa the saddle! You're old enough, Bella, to know you can't put a fire out by wavin' your hat. You got to grind that soft stuff out of your system!"

Bella said at long last, "What could Alvord do?"

"He could throw a scare into him."

"And if the scare didn't work?"

Charlie Moore sent his butt pinwheeling toward the ashes.

"There's just two things you've got to make up your mind—"

"That wasn't what I asked you."

Their eyes met and locked. The range boss flung out his hands. "If the scare don't work he'll have to start deliverin'—Now wait! Keep your shirt on. That doesn't have to mean—"

"Never mind the sugar coating." Bella's jaw turned stubborn. "I won't have Dallas killed."

"Who's talkin' about killin' him? Cripple a few of them night-ridin' bastards an' the rest'll roll cotton hell west an' crooked. Scatter that coyote pack he runs with an' Dallas—"

"All right," she said. "Go get him."

TWO

Burt Alvord

But it wasn't to prove that easy.

Charlie Moore had a lot of perseverance, but when he rode into the Bar 6 yard in the shank of an evening six days later he was just about ready to call it quits. He looked his age when he dragged into the house and shook a disgruntled head at Bella.

"No soap," he growled, dropping into a chair. "Most obstinate maverick I ever pitched rope at."

"What did he say?"

"Just grinned at me mostly. They got a poker game goin' at the Oriental—one of them supers from Willcox is in it tryin' to wear him down to where he'll pin that damn breed's tin on his shirt. Game started four night ago an' him an' this super has been playin' steady, livin' off beer an' bar snacks. They was still goin' strong when I got all I could—"

"But didn't he say anything? He must have given you some reason."

"Reason!" Moore snorted. "He give me choice of a dozen! The guy's flush right now—he ain't lookin' for work."

Without turning from the stove Bella lifted a

19

pot lid, peered, and put it back. "What did you tell him?"

The range boss scowled. "I did manage to mention we was havin' rustler troubles. But when a guy's wrapped up in a siege with the pasteboards it ain't the best time in the world to auger with him.

"About a hour 'fore I left I caught him in the can. Told him about the rustlin' an' the five men we lost. He just waved it away. 'Cow work!' he says. 'How the hell can a cow ranch compete with the county? Them boys up at Willcox is wantin' me bad. Coupla more nights of this game an' that super'll be ready to cough up his larynx.'

" 'There's things more precious than money,' I tells him, figurin' to bait my line up with you. 'Bar 6—' I says, an' there's where he chopped me off. 'Petticoat spread!' he sneers, lookin' plumb disgusted. 'I wouldn't work for no woman if I was down t' eatin' mule chips!' "

"He said that?" Bella turned.

"Hope to die if he never. An' looked like he meant every last dang word of it." The old man wrapped up the makings. "No use to count none on that feller."

Bella's eyes looked almost black in that light. She seemed to square her shoulders. She turned back to the stove. But after a moment she said above the rattling, "So he doesn't like women."

20

"Likes 'em well enough in their place, I reckon."

"In a bed, I suppose you mean."

Old Charlie looked shocked. He waggled his head.

Bella said, still fussing with the things on the stove, "I can get him."

Moore got out of his chair like a thunderclap. "I ought to wash your mouth out!"

She turned then, considering him, her green eyes crinkling humorously. "An old buck like you!" she said, and clucked her tongue at him, grinning. "Now let's be practical, shall we? Last week, by your tell of it, we had to have Alvord—"

"Jumpin' jackstraws, girl! I wa'n't figurin' to . . . to—" Roan cheeked, he spluttered to a floundering stop.

"Perhaps not," Bella smiled, "but you were counting on my appearance to pull him into this deal. I don't see that it's any worse to put my . . . ah, self where he'll be able to get an eyeful."

She curled red lips provocatively, spun around in a way that made her skirts lift a little.

Old Moore groaned. He mopped his face and glared at her. "You can't go into no barroom!"

"He's still taking nourishment, isn't he?"

"You got more in your mind than goin' to any hash house—"

"So what if I have?"

"I tell you, by grab, it ain't decent, Bella!"

21

"What isn't?"

"What you're fixin' to do—bait a trap with yourself just to fetch that guy out here."

Bella lifted her chin. "Where's the harm in my going along to have a little talk with him?"

No harm in talking, but it wouldn't stop with talk—not if he was any judge at reading folks' expressions. She saw Burt's refusal in the light of a challenge. Woman grown and brash with youth's damned confidence, she looked forward to trying out her wiles on the fellow and a roughneck like Alvord was no guy for that stuff. Burt wasn't the kind to stop short of a bed.

Had he left it there Bella might have gone no further than what amounted to speculation; but having put Burt Alvord in her head in the first place, Charlie took the view he'd got to talk her out of it. So now, in the tone of Moses handing down the Ten Commandments, he said disparagingly, "The guy's hardly better than a squaw man. Takes up with a diff'rent Mexican chippy every time he gets hold of enough cash to jingle. He's a frowsty, connivin' pool-playin' saddle bum with no more conscience than a proud-cut stud! You keep away from him—hear me?"

Bella eyed him a moment, then said with a chuckle, "Any man John Slaughter'd trust is good enough for me."

Using his own words against him, by God!

A chit like her, not even dry behind the ears yet.

Her eyes poked fun at him. "You can't have your cake and eat it, too. He's either a man to ride the river with or a dadburned two-legged skunk—make your mind up."

Charlie gave her a caustic stare and let his breath out. He didn't know what to say, hardly. The more he'd talked the worse it got; so now, when he should have talked, he decided to keep his mouth shut.

Clapping on his hat he abruptly headed for the door.

Tombstone, that in its palmiest days had been a hell-roaring metropolis of 15,000, had now been whittled away to the proportions of a ghost town where less than 600 souls still hung on for the predicted comeback. The mines had been flooded out, the surrounding hills had been gutted and the roistering, loud-talking sporting element had followed the hardrock men to Pearce and Bisbee. There was little left in Tombstone but the glory of vanished yesterdays.

The old buildings of course, in varying stages of decrepitude, still flanked the most of the all-but-forgotten thoroughfares, many of which had become grassed over and were now being grazed by scrawny cattle in pitiful mimicry of the trade supporting Willcox. Allen Street, as Bella reined into it, still showed some life in the persons of a trio of sunbonneted housewives toting home filled baskets from a trip to the general store. And there were perhaps a dozen cowponies dozing hipshot at tie rails in the full white glare of the noontime sun.

Her thoughts turned backward as she approached the Can Can, its arcaded front all but ready to collapse. She could remember this town when it was cramjammed with people, solid lines of ore wagons lifting the yellow dust hat high and shootings so common no one even bothered to learn who the corpse was.

It was hard to believe the bottom had fallen out, that the batwing doors of the Alhambra yonder weren't about to bulge to the thrust of shoulders, that this extraordinary hush could long continue unmarred by the thundering crash of sixshooters.

It made her vaguely uncomfortable to see the town so, to realize these changes, so apparent on every hand, marked the passing of an era. The free and easy gusto of the lavish past was gone, forever vanished with the people who had given the town its flavor. This wasn't the home of the Earps and the Clantons; it was only the ghost of a reckless past. And a pretty bedraggled looking ghost at that.

She rode two blocks past her destination before the boarded-up front of the Bird Cage pulled her out of her preoccupation. Where now were the lusty denizens of yesterday—the Ringos and Leslies, the Dick Clarks and Brannons, the Curly Bills and Doc Hollidays? Eighteen years of whooping and hollering and what was to show for it? Where now was their pride?

It was a sobering thought and one which, had she followed it, might have cast a different light on her own problems. But her attention, gone ahead and to the left of where Allen crossed 6th, had become engrossed in the huddle of structures formerly known as "the cribs." Bella could remember when no decent woman would have dreamt of crossing Allen or going within gunshot of this disreputable corner lest some inebriated fool mistake her for Little Gertie the Gold Dollar, Crazy Horse Lil or some other of their ilk.

Reining her horse about she headed back toward Rotten Row. Most of the ponies she'd seen were still at the racks before the Crystal Palace and the Oriental. A pair of blue-jeaned men came out and mounted and the Oriental's owner, waving a friendly hand, crossed the dust of the street and passed into the Cosmopolitan. She caught the rumble of wheels and saw the stage come in and pull up with a squeal of brake blocks just west of the O. K. Corral.

Passing the Alhambra she kneed her gelding toward the plank walk and hitch rack before the Cosmopolitan. She had no means of knowing where Alvord would eat but this place was handiest and the only hotel in Tombstone which

25

was still dishing up a meal worthy of the name. She had changed in the brush a couple miles south of town and now wore a buckskin riding skirt which fit snug at the hips without being blatant. Her low-cut blouse of white silk was pretty daring and she'd no more under it than decency required.

With her chin-thonged sombrero at a jaunty angle she stepped into the hotel and saw the clerk look twice before he got his smile to working.

The manager came forward and reached out a hand. "Haven't seen you in a coon's age. How's things at the ranch?" He had a hard time keeping his eyes on her face. "Charlie tells me you folks have been losing some cattle."

"Yes, and five hands," she said. "Burt Alvord eat here?"

"Did yesterday."

"Is that card game still going?"

"Broke up a couple hours ago."

"If he happens to come in will you see that I get to know it?"

His face didn't change but she felt color touch her cheeks. He inclined his head, said "Certainly," and she went stiffly into the dining room, too uncomfortably aware of the trend of his thinking. She halfway wished she hadn't come, but she was darned if she was going to back out now.

The big room lacked considerable of being

26

filled. There were eight or ten diners, mostly townsmen, scattered among the tables; three or four were industriously chomping toothpicks while they rummaged open copies of the locally printed *Epitaph*. The lifting glances of the others revealed surprise and a quickening interest as she moved toward a place set against the far wall. She could sense the turning of heads and, as she reached for a chair, a pudgy hand with red hairs on the backs of its fingers dexterously hauled it out with a flourish.

She smiled at the hearty-faced man in the brown derby and allowed him to seat her, thereafter removing fringed gauntlets and meticulously smoothing them as though entirely unaware of his continued existence. When he failed to take the hint and, with a flash of gold teeth, said, "The name is Haynes—" she looked up from beneath long lashes and in a voice she was sure would carry asked: "Garden tools or corsets?"

The drummer went red to his ears and departed.

Several of the gentlemen around her snickered and a couple of the news hounds lowered their papers. She gave her order to the waiter and took off her hat, hanging it to the side of her chair by its chin strap. She tucked a stray lock in place and smilingly shook her head when one of the other men held up his paper.

A pair of dudes came in looking trail-worn and weary as though they'd just got off the stage. The older man saw her and nudged his companion who shaped. a soundless whistle as they dropped into chairs beside the disgruntled drummer.

Bella reckoned her appearance was effective enough.

But what if Burt Alvord failed to eat here this noon? What if he had gone someplace else or left town?

She heard the door slam again, the clomp of spurred boots.

A tall and weather-scrinched man in a Texas-style stetson and a here-I-come suit of maroon-and-white checks moved into the room laughingly followed by two fellows in range clothes. The second of these three broke off in mid-laugh as his eyes, touring the room, collided suddenly with Bella. They moved toward the next table, the big fellow still watching her.

She thought of him as big, though he was not so big really; it was an impression he created with little basis in actual measurements. He was not, she decided, so tall as the man in the sporty checks, nor as broad as the presumptuous drummer. It might have been his proximity to the wiry third of this trio which made one think of him as big; or it might have been his manner.

She recognized the first man—the one in the glad rags—for Bill Downing, a reputedly prosperous rancher who had a cow spread over around Willcox someplace. The bottom third of his face ran mostly to bristle in the form of an overlarge and sweeping black handlebar mustache. He tossed his headgear at a hat tree and, looking around, pulled out a chair.

Bella scarcely glanced at the third of this group save to note that he was slight, had extremely curly hair and a something about his build and cast of countenance which hinted of Mexican blood in his background.

It was the big fellow who interested Bella, with his bold and lively manner so vibrantly matching the confident assurance of level gray eyes. He didn't have any gun belt strapped about him and, unlike Downing, wore his baggy-kneed pants with their bottoms outside his boot tops and a watch chain suspended across his middle that looked large enough to be attached to an anchor. His gray cotton shirt was heavily wrinkled at shoulders and elbows. A flowing white cravat was carelessly tied in a bow at his throat and a half-filled sack of Durham bulged the lower lefthand pocket of his open black cloth vest.

He was obviously a riding man though he did not have that drawn-fine rangy do-or-die look which characterized those who rode for old Charlie. There was a heavy-seeming softness about him as though he and hard work had never got acquainted; yet he looked capable enough.

There was, she thought critically, too much flesh on his face, though she could see how a lot of women might consider him handsome. She decided "fascinating" was probably the best descriptive word for him. He had heavy black brows and a black mustache cropped short at the corners of a firm good-humored mouth. His age she guessed to be in the early thirties. She watched him turn away to answer some remark from Downing about range conditions in the Sulphur Springs Valley.

The waiter came in with her food on a tray and, as he bent to place the dishes before her, he said under his breath, "You was waitin' to know about Alvord, ma'am. That's him over yonder with the cavalry-creased black hat on."

Excluding the drummer there was only one other man in the room with a hat on—the big fellow talking to Downing.

"Why, he isn't even packing a gun!" she exclaimed.

"Don't you worry about that, ma'am. He'll have hold of one almighty quick if the need comes."

THREE

"You Tell That Old Rooster"

She pecked at her food, hardly conscious of what was going into her mouth, thoughts pulled first one way and then, incredibly, another. She was, as Charlie would have said, "in a great sweat"—a long way from certain that she wanted to go on with this.

When the notion had come to her, there in the kitchen of the Bar 6 ranch house, it had all seemed so laughably easy, a simple progression in cause and effect.

Now, with the man sitting practically in reach of her, the process took on a very different aspect. This was not the grubby clown her imagination had pictured. Burt Alvord in the flesh was a four-dimensional figure, not the straw man put together from slabs and dashes of rumor but a forceful personality whose glance and self possession she found more than a little disquieting.

Not a man to be stalked with impunity.

Even viewed in the light of what she had heard there was much about Alvord to surprise and alarm her. Easy going he looked until you studied his eyes, the forward sweep of that jaw.

She had readied herself to meet a swaggering gun toter and there he sat with not a gun on him. That air of assurance, that negligent ease which had first taken hold of her awakening notice, was no practiced pose but the fruit of knowledge implemented by experience. Here was a man who knew how to take care of himself.

His notions of humor might be unrefined but she glimpsed depths in Burt Alvord not generally conceded. Watching him now as he sat listening to Downing, she sensed the hidden edges of what Slaughter must have seen. She had pictured a boisterous ruffian; it was difficult to reconcile the man with the story Moore had told about that wrestling match at Bisbee.

Remembering the stories she felt inclined to doubt her judgment. Her need, as related to Dallas, was crowding her; but could she discount the preponderance of evidence against it in favor of an impression she had acquired in a matter of minutes? To accept both you had to believe this man a bundle of contradictions so outlandishly unlikely as to seem downright ridiculous.

Her mind rebelled against imagining any such character.

Their food had come now and Downing and the wiry man were carrying on a muttered conversation to which Alvord, if he were listening, was contributing very little. She was gratified to notice that, as Moore had jocularly conceded he might, Burt was eating with his knife and using his bread for a pusher.

This made Bella feel more at ease and she began to wonder what he would do if her napkin should suddenly slide onto the floor. In the stories she'd read ladies dropped their kerchiefs but she reckoned a napkin might serve the same purpose. Alvord was seated sidewise to her with the wiry man facing her and Downing across from him. Elaborately casual, Bella reached for the bottle of sauce beyond her dishes and the napkin obligingly tobogganed to the floor.

For several moments nothing happened. Alvord continued knifing grub to his face. Then the wiry man's glance swung to Bella and lingered. He put the flat of one hand to the table, half rising. But Alvord, still chomping, dropped a big fist over it and the wiry man, scowling, sank back into his chair.

Bella's heart gave a leap. She waited, suddenly fearful, suddenly racked with impatience, but the big man continued shoveling peas to his mouth and the napkin remained where it was on the floor.

With a flush of annoyance Bella was about to reach after it when she caught Alvord watching from the corners of his eyes. It was then she recalled how she had dressed for this occasion.

She was more amused than embarrassed. His

guile in the matter inclined to restore her faith in the efficacy of rumor. It tended also to prove that he was not unmindful of her.

She settled back in her chair and went on with her dinner.

Alvord, still with his hat on, got up and came over. "I expect this is yours," he grinned, placing the crumpled square of cloth on the table.

She affected surprise, took a look at her lap and brought her eyes up, smiling. "I'm much obliged, Mister . . ."

"Alvord," he supplied. "Don't believe I've seen you round here, have I?"

"It isn't likely," she smiled. "I just arrived a little while ago."

"Big improvement." He eyed her boldly. "Figurin' to hang an' rattle here?"

"Do you think it would be worth my while?" she countered.

He loosed a deep chuckle. "I'll make out to guarantee you'd have somethin' to think back on. Mind if I set down?"

It was a purely rhetorical question. With a fine disregard of propriety he hauled out a chair and flung a hand at the waiter. " 'Nother cup of java, Joe—an' make this one know it's been over the fire." He brought his glance back to Bella. "You here by yourself?"

"That's right." Bella smiled.

"Know anyone round here?"

"I don't imagine I'd have much trouble getting acquainted."

"You can say that again!" His approving eyes took inventory. "Come in on the stage?"

"You're a great one for questions. Suppose I ask you a few?"

"Fly at it."

"I don't suppose," she said, trying to make her voice casual, "you'd be any relation to that man of your name who used to work with John Slaughter?"

He regarded her in a sharper way. "You know old John?"

"I thought we'd decided it was my turn at questions."

"Happens I'm the guy. Mind tellin' me why you wanted to know?"

"Just curious, mostly. Exciting kind of work, I'd imagine, chasing through the brush after all those hard characters; rustlers and—"

"Nothin' hard about a rustler. Seven-eighths coyote, if you want the plain truth of it. No guts to a carload. Burn a little powder an' you can't find 'em for the dust."

"They're not all like that."

He regarded her skeptically. "You by any chance one of them female writers?"

"Heavens, no!" Bella laughed. "Writing's the last thing I'd turn my hand to."

"Pretty neat hand," he said, picking up the

nearest and taking a narrowing look at the rope scalds. Their eyes locked above it and Bella's knees turned to water. It was like being confronted with a different man to catch the look of Burt Alvord now.

"You're hurting me," she said, and he let go of her hand.

"You never got them marks tryin' to play a pianner." His eyes looked cold as a pair of dead snakes. "Mebbe you'd like to tell me what the hell you think you're doin' here!"

He was mad, of course—completely loco. What other conclusion could reasonably explain his getting worked up over the mere sight of rope tracks on a stranger's palm? Loco as a sheep herder, unless. . . .

She recalled again the daring blouse she'd put on; that crack he'd made about a piano. If he'd taken her for a dancehall girl or a prospecting madam—

He got out of his chair with a face hard as granite. He put a fist on the table, leaning forward to say: "I don't know who put you onto me but you can go back an' tell 'em they're flirtin' with death." The long solid lips pulled away from his teeth. "When that stage pulls out you better be on it."

She stared at him, astounded, all the words shocked out of her. Then, as he started to turn away, an upswinging anger plowed through her and she said in a voice she could not keep from trembling: "You've no call to talk to me like that!"

Alvord grinned with his teeth. "You deny you come here lookin' for me?"

"Certainly not, but—"

"Never mind lyin'. You're a cute little trick an' I don't mind admittin' you took me in for a minute, but I wasn't weaned yesterday. Nor the day before, neither! You—"

He broke off as his friends drifted up from their table. "What's the trouble?" Downing said.

Alvord scowled, then laughed shortly. "This trick was tryin' to run a cold—"

"That's not so!" Bella cried, suddenly furious. "If you'd quit your ranting for about five seconds I'd be able to—"

"Make it good!" Alvord jeered. His glance flipped around to the thin man. "You seen her give me the come-on, Billy—you seen her work that napkin onto the floor."

The wiry man, considering her, shrugged expressive shoulders. "I thought it was a accident—"

"Well, it wasn't," Bella said. "I did it on purpose. I was trying to find some way that would give me a chance to talk with him—"

"Hear that?" Alvord said. "A put-up job. Let's git out of here, boys."

"Wait a minute," Downing grumbled, and caught hold of Alvord's arm. "We ought to give the little lady a chance to say what's on her mind—"

"She was talkin' about rustlers!"

The thin man and Downing swapped looks across his shoulder.

"What's so terrible about that?" the thin man asked seriously. "Lotsa people talkin' about cow thieves any more."

Alvord, narrowly considering him, swung a glance at Bella. They all looked at Bella. Alvord said, "Never mind the window dressin'. Look at her paws."

"Rope scars," Downing said like it pained him.

The thin fellow said, "I still don't get it."

"Your head made of ivory?" Alvord scowled, disgusted. "She's on the rustle, you fool—she was tryin' to talk it up to me!"

Bella's mouth dropped open. "Is that what you thought?"

"Too bad," Alvord jeered, "the Bird Cage ain't still goin'. With your talents, lady, you could pack the house every night in the week. Come on," he growled at Downing, "let's split the breeze."

"One moment," the thin man said, stepping forward. "I think you've made a mistake, Burt. She's too well bred to—"

"What's breedin' got to do with it?"

"I mean she's too good lookin' to have to get her dough that way."

"You seen her hands!"

Bella stared with mixed emotions from one to the other of them. It was incredible these men should be discussing her in this fashion. She said, hardly knowing whether to laugh or get mad again, "This whole thing's preposterous. I came here intending to offer Alvord a job—"

"Just what he said," Downing nodded. "A job rustling cattle—"

"That's ridiculous!" Bella flared. "They're already being rustled; what I wanted him to do was *stop* it. Can't you understand plain English? The cattle I'm talking about are *mine*."

The three men swapped looks. Alvord snorted. "She'll be tellin' us next she owns a ranch—"

"I *do* own a ranch! If you don't care to take my word for it, ask—" She broke off to send an aggravated glance about the room but the rest of the customers seemed to have swabbed plates and gone; all, that is, save the derby-hatted drummer. He had his elbows on the table like a cat at a rat hole. "Ask the clerk," she said, "or go ask Benton, the manager!"

The thin man appeared to think well of the notion and looked about to take it up when Downing shoved a hand out. "Where is this place?"

"In Guadalupe Canyon."

A subtle change came over the slant of the tall rancher's cheeks. The thin man stood as though turned to stone and Alvord's lips barely moved though his low husky voice reached her plainly enough. "Whereabouts in Guadalupe?"

"Just north of the Line—"

"Bar 6," the big man nodded; and his eyes, suddenly shifting, settled bleakly on the drummer. "You got a stake in this talk?"

The man scowled. "If you don't want it listened to—"

"Go on," Alvord said. "Drag your pin. Roll your cotton." The drummer looked inclined to bluster.

Alvord started toward him and he cleared out in a hurry.

Swinging back to face the girl, Alvord said with a chuckle, "Guess you're Bella Norton then. Expect you'll be figurin' I'm considerable of a fool, but I swear I never thought to be bumpin' into you, ma'am. Like to have you meet these fellers. This tall drink's Bill Downing from up around Willcox. Skinny one's Billy Stiles, a anti-godlin numbskull that's follered more cows' tails than any guy you'll meet in a coon's age. Boys, shake hands with Bella Norton."

Bella, mollified, put her hand out and got firm grips from both of them. Alvord settled a hip on a corner of the table and swung the hoisted leg the way a kid would. "So you're Bella Norton an'

40

you come to look me up because you're havin' rustler troubles. You spoken to the sheriff?"

"What good would that do?"

"You don't think he'd try to stop it?"

"He couldn't spend all his time at Bar 6."

Alvord nodded. "Somethin' in that. You got any idea where your stock's been goin' to?"

"All we know is that it's going—"

"Pretty near bound to have a little trouble that way, considerin' the location," Downing said. "Smugglers an' rustlers been usin' that pass for years."

"There's more back of it than that. We've always been up against some odds and ends of stealing, but nothing like this. Besides, we've lost five hands within the space of two months—"

"You mean," Stiles asked, "they plain up an' quit?"

"Shot out of their saddles," Bella said.

Alvord frowned. "Sounds kind of like someone's figurin' to run you out of there. You feudin' with anyone?"

Bella shook her head.

"Been losin' your cows in bunches?"

"Thirty to fifty head at a time."

Downing swore. "That can amount to a lot of cattle."

"If it isn't stopped soon, according to my range boss, we're going to have to sell out. Though I—"

"This range boss," Stiles said. "Don't suppose he's got a hand in this, do you?"

"Charlie Moore?" Alvord said: "Hell, no—not old Charlie; he's straight as a string. How long's it been goin' on?" he asked Bella.

She'd been expecting the question but that didn't make it any more palatable. This was harrowing ground too close for comfort but she couldn't find any satisfactory way around it.

"About ten weeks."

Stiles and Downing swapped looks again. Downing said, "That would be right after your Paw's will was probated." He appeared about to add some pertinent afterthought but after scrinching up his mouth let the thing stand as stated.

Bella's glance switched to Alvord. "If I could talk to you privately—"

"Nothin' you say is goin' to go any farther. Put your cards on the table."

Bella said reluctantly, "We're afraid my brother Dallas is back of it. He and Dad didn't often take the same view of anything and, when he discovered his share of the estate was fifty dollars, he felt very bitter."

"Figured you an' Charlie'd talked him down to your Dad?"

"He said a lot of wild things."

"You better go to the sheriff," Bill Downing advised. "He's—"

"But don't you see that's the one thing I can't do? My own brother! Surely—"

"You rather lose the place?" That was Stiles. She didn't answer.

Alvord frowned at her, puzzled. "What'd you think I could do?"

"It was Charlie's idea. He thought you might be able to throw a scare into him—"

"Oh, he did, did he?" Alvord got off the table with his eyes like agate. "Lovely spot I'd be in if someone put the fool's light out! You tell that old rooster I ain't huntin' rope collars!"

FOUR

Neck Meat or Nothing

Bella considered him in the silence of pure astonishment.

She'd been prepared to encounter resistance. But in the light of Charlie's high regard for his prowess it hadn't entered her mind Alvord might refuse the job on the grounds of imagined risk.

She looked at him carefully, wondering if the fellow was laying pipe for a belly laugh, but could find no sign of it in the cold hard depths of that unwinking stare.

"Are you serious?"

"You ever find anythin' funny in the sight of a guy with his neck stretchin' hemp?"

"But that's unreasonable," she said. "I don't want him shot. All we want you to do is—"

"You ain't talkin' to me."

"All right, leave that out. You don't have to threaten him. You needn't even go near him. Just sign on with Bar 6 to help us stop that rustling."

Alvord shook his head.

Bella's lip curled a little. "I've heard it said you were yellow but I didn't believe it."

"No skin off my nose what you believe."

Bella felt like striking him. It was unthinkable

45

to have come all this way and gone so far with it only to have the whole thing fold up in her face. She gave him a look none who called themselves men should be able to endure without it came from their wives, but Alvord grinned mockingly.

She wet her lips with her tongue. She dropped a glove; was bending to retrieve it, flushing, when he said, "No use to strain yourself, sugar. You done everything but put it on the line an' I ain't bitin'. If Charlie's bound to git his ashes raked there's plenty guys hangin' round this burg that can be propositioned for half what you're offerin'."

She was so riled she couldn't get enough breath to speak with. Alvord patted her shoulder. "Cheer up, baby. Night's always blackest just before the sun gits up. Come on," he said to the others, "let's drift."

He beckoned the waiter. "Count this lady in, too." He dropped six cartwheels in the man's hand and left them. He was entering the lobby when Billy Stiles said guardedly: "How much would that job be worth to you, ma'am?"

Bella checked a rash impulse. Looked him over again. "You really think you could do it? I'm afraid he's made his mind up—"

"Him? I couldn't do nothin' with him—hell, no. What I was figurin', if the price stacks right I might take a whack at this deal myself."

She regarded him indifferently. It was Charlie's

emphasized notion there was only one man could do up this chore, and that fellow's name was Alvord—not that Bella was entirely convinced; but when she heard the slam of the hotel door she made herself look at Stiles with a little more care.

He didn't cut much ice when stacked up against her seething recollections of Alvord. He looked too puny, too young and too friendly—too much like the kind you'd always find riding grubline whenever there was reason to cut down on hired help.

"I don't know," she said, considering. "When my brother gets on his high horse he can be a pretty hard man to handle."

"Thought you told Burt he could leave Dallas out of it; that what you wanted mainly was to get that cow stealin' stopped?"

"Well, but—"

"Billy'll make you a first class hand," Downing said, coming back from the cigar case. "Knows a heap about cows an' been around all over."

"But I'm not hunting a cowboy. What I need is a man who can deal with those rustlers."

"What I meant," Downing nodded, biting the end off his stogy. "I'm not sayin' he's better than Alvord, but he ain't far behind him. Knows this country like the palm of his hand. Spent a season ridin' shotgun for Wells Fargo, same as Burt done. Reads sign like a Injun. We had him workin' one time for the Cowmen's Association.

Don't let his size misguide you. He can be rough as a cob."

Bella looked dubious.

"Knows the law angles, too. He's constable over to Pearce—"

"What in the world is he doing here then?"

"To tell you the God's unadulterated truth," Stiles grinned, "I got them long-haired loafers so whipped down you couldn't get one to spit on the floor of a backhouse."

"That's right," confirmed Downing, cupping fire to his smoke. "You can hear them Pearce beds creak every time a guy turns over."

"But I'm afraid," Bella said, "this bunch that's after my cattle haven't very much in common with a town of Cornish miners. Understand," she told Billy, "I'm not saying you couldn't do it, but—"

"You're givin' his size too much of your notice," Downing warned. "You got a feller here that knows how to work a rifle an' that's the first thing you need when you're declarin' war on rustlers. Big names ain't goin' to stop 'em. Muscle's no good to you. Hot lead's the only thing you'll ever get to stop a cow thief."

"An' if you don't get someone quick," Stiles said, "you won't have no cows left to rustle."

Something about that crack didn't set too well with Bella, but his good-natured face held no hint of guile and she finally shrugged it off, putting it down to imagination. Downing was an experienced rancher. He would hardly recommend Stiles the way he had without he was satisfied the man was as good as she was likely to get hold of.

"All right," she smiled, "I'll hire you, Billy. Can you ride out there with me now or will you have to go back to Pearce first?"

"I ain't worryin' none about Pearce," Stiles said. "What I'm wantin' to know is how much will this pay me?"

"Can't we decide that later?"

"I'd feel better knowin' now. No use for me to go out there if I can't do no better'n make day wages."

That didn't set too well with Bella, either, though she understood that her feelings were unreasonable in the light of the risk the man was bound to be taking. She said, "How much do you want?"

Stiles whacked his hat against his leg with a grin. "You goin' to bargain with your future?" He could see she didn't like that. He tried to smooth it over. "After all, they're your cattle. How much you figure it's worth?"

He had an unhappy faculty of tossing around bits of painful truth and, though it made her inwardly furious, Bella showed considerable fortitude in managing to keep hold of her temper. As he had so crustily pointed out, if she didn't get this rustling stopped pretty quick she would soon be stripped down to where she couldn't even sell what was left of the outfit.

"Name your price," she said grimly. "If it's too far out of line I'll let you know."

Stiles rasped his chin. "I ain't too partial to gettin' paid by the job—kind of like to have somethin' to be goin' along with. In a deal like this if I collect once a week I won't be left grabbin' leather if you should pitch in your hand."

He considered her a moment with his tongue licking across one corner of his mouth. He took a deep breath. "I'd want a hundred a week."

Bella said, angry: "I'm not running a bank."

"Well . . . seventy-five then."

Bella started for the door.

"No sense gettin' mad," Stiles grumbled, hastening after her. "I got my hide to think about—will you pay me fifty?"

"Your hide's not worth fifty," Bella said scornfully. "I'll give you two steers a week. Take it or leave it."

"You'd play hell gettin' Alvord for any such price!"

"You're not Alvord," she said; and Billy Stiles shrugged resignedly.

"Okay. Keep your hair on while I go fetch my horse."

FIVE

Star Packer

When Burt Alvord stepped off the hotel porch onto the roweled plank walk flanking the south side of Allen he had things on his mind besides his Cavalry-creased stet hat. He'd been intending after eating to fork his horse and head for Willcox but he didn't know now what the hell he'd better do.

Scrinching his eyes against the glare he swiveled a cursory glance at the daydreaming horse racked beyond the Cosmopolitan's steps. He ducked under the rail and had a look at its brand.

Bar 6, all right.

He went on across the street and stepped up under the wooden awnings, more dissatisfied than ever. He'd had little to do with Old Man Norton and wanted no truck with Dallas or Bella, but there were angles to this thing he couldn't afford to ignore. That girl was a menace any way you took her.

Still scowling, he turned west and struck out with his thoughts toward the O. K. Corral. He crossed the dust of Fourth, passed the broken-windowed front of the abandoned Can Can,

51

and the farther he went the darker his face got. Willcox was the place for him and the sooner he got over there the better he was going to like it.

He turned into the Corral's big open-fronted barn but, after standing a moment in frowning thought, he swung around and went back for another look at the street.

Supposing that dratted girl should hire Stiles!

This might normally have fetched a great laugh out of Alvord but he was too uneasy to find humor in anything. Keeping back out of sight he was presently watching Stiles step out of the Cosmopolitan. The girl wasn't with him. Bill Downing wasn't, either.

Growing steadily more dissatisfied he watched Stiles cross to the upper side of Allen, turn north up Fourth and pass from view beyond the Can Can. Alvord wheeled, turning away and as abruptly turning back again, eyes narrowing down to little better than gleaming cracks. By God he didn't like this! What devil's work was that old fool up to?

Sweat cracked through Burt Alvord's skin as he stood there considering the pair in conjunction; the girl with her lack of any worthwhile experience and the purple-nosed Texican who hadn't owned an honest thought since he'd got himself up and climbed out of the cradle.

Stiles, at least to Burt, generally called him Sam Bass because of the endless tales he was forever recounting of the days when he had ridden with that notorious outlaw. Alvord would have scoffed at these except for one thing; going over a couple of train jobs one night while in his cups Downing had come out with details no one could have imagined who hadn't actually been a participant—he had even let go of his right name at last and Burt could no longer doubt him.

Alvord cursed the whole setup. That Norton skirt was a pretty smart pigeon but a hell of a long ways from being smart as she figured. And there was no good closing his eyes to her, not with Charlie Moore looking over her shoulder. The old bastard's gun may have got a clogged barrel but there wasn't no rust in his think-box.

With such notions juning round inside him, Alvord was about to slip his pin and go down there when Downing came out and went across to the Oriental. The screen slapped again and there was Bella Norton with her knees against the railing. She took a head-swinging look up and down the length of Allen, came around the tie rail and swung up into her saddle with a flash of white leg before she got her pony settled and that leather skirt pulled down. Then, instead of riding, she just sat there.

She made an eye-filling picture with the breeze plastering that go-to-hell blouse against the front of her. Ordinarily such a sight would have quickened Alvord's pulses, but his mind kept dragging up the face of Old Charlie and the look of his cheeks got darker and darker.

Was that vinegarroon fishing or was he baiting a trap with her?

It could make a lot of difference. In the old days Moore had been a pretty tough monkey in charge of an outfit so salty not even Bill Brocius had cared to get its dander up. But that was in the faroff past and Charlie's crew today lacked a lot of measuring up to it. Though it was still one of the biggest working cow spreads in the county, time had made its inevitable changes and the men on its payroll were average hands with neither the bounce nor savvy to whip off what was happening to it. So the play boiled down to whether Charlie was actually desperate or sitting back and trying out a long-odds hunch for size.

Meantime Willcox was waiting. A hundred a month the commissioner had promised and if he wanted to collect it Burt had better get a move on.

Staring into the sunlit glare of the street he couldn't think why he kept dawdling. The chances stacked up around a thousand to one Moore was down to rock bottom and trying to hire on the toughest gun he could get.

That made sense but it didn't convince Alvord.

Charlie Moore wasn't the kind to beg favors from anyone. And, after being turned down in the first place, it wasn't in keeping for him to send in this girl got up to look the way she had without there was a heap more behind it than was showing on the surface.

He turned again toward his horse and once again stopped, swearing. He was being seven kinds of a fool and knew it. A spread on the skids was very like a bruised apple and he sure wasn't craving any truck with a woman—not, anyways, with Bella Norton's kind. He liked his fun where he found it and didn't want it cropping up in terms of the hereafter. Yet, if it hadn't been for Charlie so plainly breathing down her neck. . . .

He shook his head and scowled streetward.

There, by God, at last she was moving.

And then he swore bitterly.

Stiles had joined her, coming out of an alley; and she was turning her horse, riding off with the fellow, the pair of them heading in the direction of Bar 6!

A quorum of the town fathers met as soon as it was learned Burt had finally got to Willcox. He was unceremoniously routed from a corner saloon and fetched before this august body, more commonly known as the "Vigilance Committee." The Chairman reviewed the current situation. Willcox, he said, had become a tough problem. A rowdy cattle element, composed of whooping gun-shooting cow hands, took over the place every time they rode in. They came on the gallop, roping stray dogs and pedestrians. No decent woman dared be seen on the streets. Still, these fellows were good customers and, if they could be toned down a little, the town was willing to put up with them for the sake of the cash they pushed over its counters.

"We want them controlled," the Chairman explained, "but not to the point where they'll take their trade elsewhere. We got a lot of confidence in your ability to keep this bunch of damn fools in line."

Burt looked him in the eye. "Let me get this straight. I'm to be a kind of rep for your Mexican constable—that right?"

The Chairman looked a little fussed. This was sort of a delicate subject on account of the Texas element, which made up a large part of the locality's population, would sooner be found dead than take orders from a Mexican. Burt, on the other hand, was known to have been on fairly close terms to a recently deceased long-looper named Eduardo Lopez who'd done a moving business in Mexican cattle. If Burt could chum round with a guy of that name the Committee saw no reason why he couldn't just as well work awhile with the fellow who was packing their tin.

Of course the Chairman didn't put it that bluntly. He said, "It probably wouldn't be for more than a couple of weeks. If you can hold this bunch down we'll probably make you the marshal."

Burt picked up his hat. "I can't do business on 'probably.' "

The Chairman hastened to assure him he could count on it. Definitely. "You got to remember the guy's been elected. We can't just up an' throw him out of the job."

"You want firearms prohibited inside the town limits?"

"So far as this cow crowd's concerned. And a curfew. I'd admire to get a little sleep for a change."

"Anything else?"

"We're not tying your hands. Consistent with keeping their business, the main thing we're after is control—some security. We want the racket kept down and this rowdyism stopped. There's seven damn fools from the Bud Hood Ranch carryin' on in Schweitzer's saloon right now."

Burt scowled and shifted his weight and said finally: "What if I have to kill three or four of these birds?"

"Go ahead and kill them—that's what we're hirin' you for."

"Okay," Alvord grunted, "I'll take the job. What's the first thing you want ironed out?"

"Go down to Schweitzer's and disarm those cowprodders. Get it through their heads this town's fed up with their goddam horseplay and that from here on out personal property'll be protected."

This was quite a large order. These same seven cowboys had been whooping things up and defying the Committee and its Mexican badge toter for the past three days and nights hand-running. And, on top of that, the Bud Hood outfit, which headquartered across the line in Sonora, had one of the saltiest reputations of any spread in the country and its foreman, Cowboy Bill, was a notorious gun thrower whose skill was considered little short of Buckskin Frank Leslie's when that deadly marksman had been at his best.

Burt gave them a scowl and clanked out to his horse. He strapped on his shell belts, pinned on his new star, rode over to the saloon and quietly stepped inside. The Bud Hood boys had the place to themselves and were riding the bartender high wide and handsome.

Alvord shucked his lefthand persuader, looked the bunch over and said, grimly smiling, "You're lookin' at the new deputy constable, gents. Some of you birds'll remember me from Pearce. Them as don't can have a demonstration. Now git busy an' unbuckle."

Dropped belts hit the floor in a series of thuds.

"Step back," Alvord nodded.

Not a word was said while he gathered their gear.

"You can pick these up at my office when you leave. Don't bring 'em back."

It was as simple as that.

The Bud Hood boys did a lot of wild talking after Burt left the premises but no jaws wagged where he was likely to hear them. They rode out of town quietly a couple of hours later and no drunken shouting disturbed Willcox that night.

The members of the Committee felt mighty pleased with themselves. They convened the next day, told the constable to resign and the following week appointed Alvord town marshal. By the end of that week the news had got around and cowboys, visiting Willcox, rode in with wrapped gun belts which they deposited with the aprons at their favorite drink emporiums, there leaving them until they were ready to pull out. Only one incident occurred that night. A lallygagging cowpoke from the Boxed BT downed a couple too many and roped the fat proprietor of the Double Star Cafe. Alvord saw it happen and promptly broke the man's arm. As an object lesson it proved mighty efficacious. So much so, in fact, that at the end of his fifth week, Alvord gave himself a holiday and rode to Bar 6.

He arrived in the afternoon. Except for the smoke coming out of the cook shack the place looked deserted. He lifted his husky voice in a yell. "Anybody home?"

An old codger popped his head out the door.

"Light down an' rest your saddle." He took a squint at the sun. "Boss and some of the boys'll be in before long. Make yourself homey."

"Miz Bella around?"

"Off with the crew—leastways, what's left of it. Ain't I seen you before?"

"Like as not," Alvord said, not much caring. He reined his buckskin over to the gate of the horse trap, got down, pulled off his gear and slapped the gelding in, afterwards putting up the bars. Heaving his kack to the top rail, he spread the damp blanket hair side out; looped his gun belts and bridle round the horn of his saddle. He was hunkered down, whittling, when the outfit rode in an hour and ten minutes later.

Charlie Moore spotted him soon as he hit the yard. He tossed his reins at a puncher and came straight over. "How's tricks?" he said. "Still marshalin' Willcox?"

"It ain't takin' up all of my time," Burt answered, aware that Bella had seen him and deliberately ignored him. "Stiles got all your rustlers run off?"

Charlie eyed him, disgusted, and eased his hind end carefully down on the step. He rolled up a smoke, ran his tongue across the paper. "He's a damn poor substitute for the guy I had in mind."

"Any more of your crew turned up with slugs in 'em?"

Moore said laconically, "No, but three's quit. What does it take to hire a man of your caliber?"

"Hell," Alvord said, "I couldn't work for no petticoat."

"You'd be workin' for me."

Burt chucked him a grin. "Same thing, once removed. Lost any more critters?"

"Stiles says not, but I ain't too sure of it. You could practically name your own price right now."

"Still figurin' the brother's behind it?"

"Who else?" Moore said.

"How old's this kid?"

"Old enough to know better."

"Older than his sister?"

"Couple or three years."

"What got the old man down on him?"

Moore sifted dirt, let it slide through his fingers. "Poor judgment. All around. First the kid's let to do any damn thing he pleases an' he pleased to do a lot of things he oughta been strapped for. Time Dave hauled him up it was too late an' too sudden. Showdown come when Dallas writes the old man's name on a check for fifteen hundred which he give to a gambler. Old man was so mad he ordered the kid off the place."

"Then what happened?"

"You been around."

"So the ol' man died an' cut him off with fifty dollars."

Burt tossed his stick aside and folded up his jackknife. "Know where your cattle been goin'?"

They traded glances for a moment.

"I couldn't prove it," Moore said.

"Ever had any trouble with this outfit above you?"

"Crazy K?" Moore's look narrowed. "Not that I know of. Kraitch offered to buy the girl out after Dave died."

"Ten cents on the dollar?"

"No, he made her a good price." He spun his butt away irritably. "Kraitch ain't gettin' those cows."

"Why'd she turn him down?"

"Sentiment, mostly."

"Could she make it pay?"

"Could if Dallas would leave her alone."

The cook yelled, "Grub!" and banged on his dishpan.

"She'd do better to sell," Burt said, getting up.

"Never figured you come out here just for the ride."

SIX

Dangerous Business

Alvord knew what he figured.

It occupied his thoughts all the time he was eating and shaped pretty much the way he'd got it sized up. On account of those Papago ponies and him giving Eduardo Lopez a little help, Charlie Moore had him pegged for a whittlewhanging rustler. Worse than that the old fool, by all the signs and signal smokes, had got it in his craw Burt was repping for Dallas and had come over here simply to make sure this was understood.

It stuck out like the tongue on a wagon.

Other things began to engage his interest.

Short of throwing his accusations straight in Burt's teeth there wasn't much Moore could do except to pile on more timber for a raise in the ante, which explained why Charlie wasn't sitting with them now. He'd be up at the house doing everything he could to get it through the girl's head their only chance of coming out depended on finding Burt's price and paying it.

Alvord turned that over, not particularly enthused but not blind to it, either. He was still engrossed when Moore tramped in and took his place at the table.

Several of the others got finished and dug up the makings. "How you findin' the ozone at Willcox?" one of them asked, looking up with a grin.

"Mild," Burt said, helping himself to more beans with a hungry man's relish.

"Better keep your eyes peeled for Cowboy Bill. Them Bud Hood boys ain't likin' you much."

"Comes to that," Burt allowed, "I ain't huggin' them, to notice."

After the crew had drifted out Moore said, reaching for the biscuits, "You're wanted up to the house soon's you've got your tapeworm quieted."

"Come in," Bella called, in answer to Burt's knock.

She'd put a dress on for him and had her hair fixed different. She had the lamp turned low but he was no more blind to the challenge of her than he'd been that day in Tombstone.

He dropped into a chair and she sat down on a sofa across from him, adjusting her skirt and coming at once to the point. "How much are you risking your life for at Willcox?"

"I'm satisfied," Burt said.

"You ought to have more ambition. You should be thinking of your future. Charlie's getting old; he won't be rodding this spread forever. If you'd tie up with Bar 6 you could step into that job—"

"At eighty a month for the rest of my natural?"

"Eighty and interest. That's worth thinking about, isn't it?"

Burt thought about it with his glance drifting down to where the cloth was pulled tight just forward of her armpits. Several moments went by before he suddenly became conscious he was sitting in a vacuum. Then Bella was saying, "Do you find it hard to hear me, Mr. Alvord?"

Grinning, Burt said, "Mebbe if I moved closer . . ." and got up and straightaway did so, unabashedly ignoring imperious eyes and lifted chin. He even had the crust to chuckle when she moved back as far as the couch's frame permitted. "What kind of interest?"

Cold stares didn't bother him, either.

At last Bella said, "Twenty per cent of the ranch's total income after running expenses and bills have been paid."

Burt shifted his weight, moving several inches nearer, while appearing to be engrossed with the complexities of mathematics. "I reckon there's guys would be mighty impressed with that sort of bait."

"You're not then, I take it?"

"I've seen things I liked better."

He was close enough now to have dropped an arm around her and she suddenly sprang up, glaring down at him, furious. "I'm trying to talk business—"

"I been hearin' you."

"If you're not interested—"

"But I am," he protested. "I can't hardly sit still!"

Bella flushed. "You know what I'm talking about; if you're so interested why don't you take it?"

"I think," he said, getting up, "I will"; and the next moment had her locked in his arms. It was not the technique she'd been accustomed to and he'd caught her by surprise, knowing she hadn't quite believed he would dare. He didn't give her the chance to throw any tantrums; she tried the next best thing and went limp as a bar rag. But she came out of that fast when his mouth found hers. She scratched like a wildcat; kicked at his ankles. Burt hung on and, incontrollably trembling, her mouth gave way underneath his rough handling and she was suddenly responding to the things he had roused, pressing fiercely against him, when the sound of spurred boots came across the porch planking.

She broke away, eyes enormous, panting, half sobbing. The muted thunder of pounding was a long continued din when Alvord, softly cursing, wheeled and strode to the door.

Charlie Moore was outside. "You people deaf?" he asked, scowling.

"We was kind of wrapped up in the terms of that agreement. Somethin' on your mind?"

"Maybe," Moore said, "I—"

"We don't need any help."

The old man's shape turned as stiff as a hayfork. Bella called through the tightening silence: "Who is it?"

"Me!" Charlie growled. "You all right in there, Bella?"

"Why, of course." She came forward. "Whatever in the world—"

"Charlie," Burt grinned, "has just about convinced himself the roof will fall in if he don't stick around to watch it."

Bella's look was puzzled. "We've just about got this settled," she told Charlie brightly. "Burt's riding over the ground first thing in the morning."

Charlie's eyes shone like the antelope's over the fireplace. "Better send him to get some sleep then. We don't keep banker's hours on this spread."

Alvord spent the best part of the next day riding; one of the hands went along to point out landmarks and boundaries, and when they got back Burt knew pretty near as much about the Bar 6 as Moore did, and considerably more about the fate of its cattle. He'd had some rather shrewd notions about those cattle all along.

After putting up his horse and giving it a graining he cuffed the dust off his clothes, splashed some water on his face and sauntered over to bang a fist on the ranch house door. The crew wasn't back and he hadn't seen Bella; he had it in his mind she might have stayed at home today.

He was right.

Appearing a trifle skittish she joined him on the porch. Burt flopped himself down on the step and grinned up at her like he never even noticed she'd neglected to ask him in.

"Reckon I'll take you up on that job," he said cheerfully. "But there's a couple of things we'd better git settled. First thing is I ain't workin' under Charlie. My time's to be my own an' I'll report direct to you."

Bella studied him curiously, careful not to mention petticoats. She said, endeavoring not to be so conscious of him, "Isn't that a bit unusual? I mean—"

"Whole deal's unusual. I've already got a job town-marshalin' Willcox. If it got out I was putting in time over here the Committee might decide to pick up my badge. That sure wouldn't suit me."

The suggestion of a frown narrowed Bella's appraisal. "I don't see how you expect to stop this rustling—"

Alvord grinned. "You just leave that to me. I figure to make them cow-grabbers hard to find. That's what you're wantin', ain't it? Just to git rid of 'em?"

Bella's probing glance seemed a little bit

dubious. "Stiles allowed he could too, but—"

"You probably ain't been makin' it enough worth his while. To git the best out of Billy you got to give him somethin' to line his sights on. Nice fat dollar sign would stir up his interest."

"I suppose by that—"

"You ain't forgettin' last night?"

Color swept into her cheeks and she said angrily: "If you're presuming to think you can trade on that—"

"Kind of figured it was you that was doin' the trading. Didn't you say if I signed on I could expect to step into Charlie's shoes when he was done with 'em?"

Bella eyed him suspiciously. "I—You mean you'll undertake to stop this rustling on that basis?"

Burt grinned admiringly. "You're a lot of woman, Bella, but I ain't riskin' my hide just to hear the chestnuts pop. You offered me that to sign on with Bar 6—and twenty per cent of the spread's net profits plus Charlie's eighty cartwheels. I'd expect somethin' extra to stop them cow thieves."

"I'm practically down to rock bottom. How much extra do you want?"

"Let's see how it turns out."

"I prefer to know what I am letting myself in for."

"Me, too," Burt nodded. "These boys might be

stubborn." The bold look of his eyes fetched her color up again. He chuckled. "No results, no pay."

"I'm not about to give you the ranch," Bella said.

"I ain't about to ask for it."

"I'm afraid I can't afford you," Bella said. "You'd better ride."

Burt stretched and got up. "It's your ranch," he grinned. "If you aim to let pay stand between yourself and stayin' in the cattle business, I reckon you'll soon be out of it."

She let him go. She let him go halfway to the stable before she stirred from her tracks. Then she went into the house.

She kept out of sight all the while he was saddling but was waiting, chin up, when he got to the gate. Eating crow was a chore she was plainly not used to but she put the best face she could on the matter. "I've thought the whole thing over and I accept your terms."

Alvord didn't quite grin but he might just as well have. "The price has got up," he said, eyeing her brazenly.

She fought hard to hold back the rush of her temper, to let him see only the contempt he had courted.

Then the chuckle burst out of him. "Decided I better have a little on account," he said and, bending from the saddle, kissed her squarely on the mouth.

• • •

The moon blanked out behind a scud of white cloud about the time Burt Alvord was riding into Willcox. He'd thought of dropping by his office but, tired with the long hours spent in the saddle, decided against it and cut across back lots in the direction of Schweitzer's. With no way of knowing what might have happened during his absence he believed the back door might be worth the extra bother.

A high board fence surrounded the rear of the saloonman's premises with a single gate leading in off the alley. He saw the dark bulk of the paling, got off his horse and was quietly leading the docile gelding through the opening when a black shape stirred like smoke in the shadows. Quicker than hell could scorch a feather a gun came up and was cocked in Burt's hand.

"*Por Dios*—don' shoot!"

It was the scared-frantic bleat of Soto's brother-in-law, the Mexican constable whom Burt had replaced. Lot of guys in his boots would have hated Burt's guts, but not this fellow; he was firmly convinced that by taking his job Burt had saved his life—and at considerable risk.

"What moves, Enrico?"

"*Sangre de Cristo*! Four-five hours I wait in these rat hole. This Bod Hood boys she's look for you. Pretty soon kill."

Burt grasped the Mexican's hand, thanked

71

him warmly while inwardly throttling down an impulse toward laughter. Those Bud Hood boys were *hombres malo* but this wolf talk of theirs had been making the rounds ever since he'd first shucked them of their irons here in Schweitzer's. At least a dozen other friends and well-wishers had warned him.

Nothing in the threat to get his bowels in an uproar but for Enrico's benefit he put some frost in his voice. "Goin' to salivate me, are they?"

The Mexican crossed himself, teeth chattering.

"Tequila talk, mebbe."

"No tequila—she's no *borracho, senor*! They 'ave cut the cards and these Cowboy Bill she 'ave pulled the deuce. Say kill you pronto. They bring in the steers for sheep on the chug-chug but no go home. These boss man say, 'If that horse-thieving son . . .' "

"Oh, he did, did he?" Burt's voice was grim in dead earnest now. This cutting of the cards was a new piece of business and he'd had some words with Cowboy Bill before. The guy had given Burt a horse when he'd been drunk awhile back, probably in the hope the new marshal would look with more tolerance on the outfit's antics. When that hadn't proved the case he'd started the word that Burt had deliberately done him out of the horse.

Burt had ignored him, which had been a mistake. He'd come armed and stayed armed on

72

his last two-three visits and, when that hadn't been challenged, had packed his bullypuss pride a little further. Buying drinks for the crowd he'd several times yanked his pistol and invited the apron to "take it outa that!"

Burt reckoned it was time he had a talk with Mr. Bill.

Strapping on his shell belts he brushed grimly past Enrico and stepped into the saloon. The Bud Hood outfit was bellying the bar but there wasn't any evidence of its gun slinging ramrod.

Burt reckoned he'd be back and took a chair at an empty table.

More than just a few things ran through his mind and when Frank Aikens pushed through the batwings Alvord shoved out a chair and beckoned him over.

"How they treatin' you?" Aikens said, folding back in it.

"I'm still managin' to eat," Alvord grunted. Leaning forward then and keeping his voice down he asked if Frank had been around for the card cut.

"Nope. But I heard about it. Bill drew low card an' blew it round pretty loud he was gonna stop your clock. I dunno where you been, Burt, but it's sure give that buck a lot of ammunition. Half this town thinks he's run you out."

Burt growled and showed his eyeballs.

Aikens slanched a covert glance in the direction

of the bar. "Better keep your eyes skinned. I wouldn't trust a one of 'em."

Burt could feel the tension mounting. Talk was thinning down and an air of expectancy had hold of men's faces. A lot of them looked wooden but there were some that weren't so guarded and four or five of the Sonorans looked downright ugly. A couple of cowmen near the bar abruptly took off like the heel flies were after them.

Aikens nodded. "There goes the word. He'll know you're here now."

"Let's make it goddam sure," Alvord said. "You'll find my bronc outside the back door. Take him over to my place an' throw the hull on that pacer. Take it round to the front an' tie the damn jughead where every guy an' his uncle can git a good eyeful."

"You think that's smart?"

"Smart or not that's how I want it. We'll see who's scarin' who around here."

Aikens shrugged and went off.

Alvord scowled. He shied a few crusty glances here and there about the room. He was engaged in this pastime when the front doors rocked into place behind a black jowled character whose uncompromising stare, plowing through the gathered assemblage, found Burt and came toward him as though there were nothing more substantial in his way than Willcox climate. This was Matt Berts whose body had jounced with

Alvord's north from Bisbee that time. He cut a swath through the crowd with uncaring elbows.

"What the hell's coming off?" He swung Aikens' chair about and straddled its seat.

"Not sure," Alvord said, "but it'll be worth waiting for."

The bartender, catching his signal, fetched over a bottle and a couple of glasses.

"Well, here's to it," Berts grinned and, downing the amber like a rinse for his tonsils, shoved back his glass for a refill.

Alvord poured and belched. "Get a look at that stuff the Bud Hood bunch just shipped?"

"Watched the last car fill. Wasn't paying much notice. Anything wrong?"

"Number of Bar 6 cows is missin'."

"Oh, for Chrissake!" Matt Berts looked pained and let his attention loop back to where the most of the racket was. "Same old sixes an' sevens. You been around this place long enough now to know—"

"More to it than that. Someone's gettin' ambitious."

Berts looked at him and snorted; then, more carefully, looked again. "How you mean?"

"Don't know—yet. I'm only sniffin' round the edges." Alvord picked up his glass, sloshed the liquor, set it down. "Tough crew our friend's roddin'. Spend a lot of time hangin' round this burg. Fellers that can spend that much time off their range can git around free enough to do most anything."

"To grab Bar 6 cattle?"

"They ain't leavin' tracks. Know anythin' about Kraitch?"

"Runs the Crazy K, don't he?"

"Ever seen him with Bill?"

Berts said, "Don't recollect it."

"Could be a tie-up there someplace. I don't say there is but you turn a bunch of cattle loose back in them draws an' they could sure be hard to find. Next time you saw 'em they might look like Bud Hoods."

"You fixing to pin this on Bud?"

"Bud wouldn't touch it. Some other gents, though, might not be so damn squeamish. Nothin' to stop 'em dealin' with Bud's rannies an' runnin' this stuff in with Bud's regular shipments—or even runnin' in a extra, with Bud's crew to handle it. Wouldn't take but three or four of 'em."

"What you got against Kraitch?"

"He's been tryin' to buy 'em out an' he's been seen two-three times south of Naco with Dallas. Also, I don't like the kind of business he's in." Alvord glanced at Berts' doodling. "What's the word on Bill Downing?"

"Living high off the hog." Berts appeared engrossed with the rings he was making on the top of the table. "No need to go out of your way to hunt trouble." He tipped his head toward the

76

bar. "Sounds like they're getting their steam up again."

Alvord raised another match to his limp cigarette and a half-amused glance slid over the edge of the hand cupped before it. "I've hired on," he said quietly, "to cut that outfit's losses."

Berts looked up from his project in circles. "Someone *is* getting proud. Hell—you trying to get planted?"

"I ain't doin' it for peanuts. Chance to clean up if the right cards is played."

"Spread was left to the girl, wasn't it?"

Alvord stifled a yawn, dropped his elbows and grinned. "Squeeze play, Matt. Nothin' wrong with me squeezin' if the chance comes my way."

"Nothing wrong with providing the chance, either, is there?"

"I could use a little help. How about you goin' over there tomorrow? Get hold of Stiles an' throw the hooks to him. Let him know I've taken chips. Tell him you're down there to keep a eye on them cattle an' that if any more is moved someone's liable to git hurt."

"He's had a pretty good thing there."

"He's had it long enough."

Berts' eyes brightened. "How far you wanting I should go with this thing?"

"All the way. I want that rustlin' stopped."

"Some of these bucks ain't going to like it. That cub, for one."

"I ain't that kid's keeper. If he's got the sense to pound sand he'll roll cotton."

Matt Berts took another good swig from the bottle. "You ain't wrong about that blood part. Chacon's in this someplace; he ain't holed up in them cedar brakes to start no trade in fence posts. My guess is them cows has been going to him. If they have I'd sooner play tag with a tiger."

The front doors skreaked and Alvord's look went away from him but returned almost at once. "Aikens," he said; and a moment later Aikens joined them.

"All set," he nodded. "I hope you got your rabbit's foot."

SEVEN

Stalking Cat

Berts' glance went curiously from one to the other of them.

Neither offered to enlighten him. Alvord said, "See him round anyplace while you was takin' that stroll?" and again Aikens nodded.

"Outside this joint right now, pawin' gravel."

Berts flung a narrowing look toward the bar, sent it raveling on to consider the batwings, shoving back his chair with a squeal of scraped legs as the doors bulged, complaining, to a sudden thrusting weight. It was only Stacey Cohen, the Double Star's fat proprietor; and Berts sank back with a resentful growl.

Aikens grinned. "Guilty conscience, Matt?"

"Scairt he might have to marry the girl," laughed a half drunk fool from the poker game yonder. Berts was minded to cuff a little care into this neighbor but, before he could stir, there was a flurry of motion, another skreak from the doors. A kind of paralysis anchored the joints of Berts' body as his wheeling stare winged down a broad lane into a pair of scrinched eyes that were like puddled iron.

The boss of the Bud Hood boys had arrived.

• • •

Matt Berts felt sweat roll down the runnels of his mouth. He'd never been so disturbed in his life. He wanted terribly to get out of there and couldn't lift a finger.

There were upwards of thirty men in the place, every last one gone still as a stovepipe. The lemon glow of the lamps accentuated everything; and a sudden creep of hope drove some of the cold from Berts' belly as he realized he was staring at a man who wasn't heeled.

It was hard to believe after all his wild talk that a man of Bill's rep could have so tamely backed down, harder still to believe he would advertise the fact by appearing here unarmed. Unless—

Again Berts felt the breath catch inside him.

The guy had a coat on, a loose thing, hanging open. Only through some trick of this long room's lighting had Matt caught the sag of that coat's off pocket.

In a flash he understood.

He flung an alarmed look across his shoulder at Alvord and was aghast, outraged by the aggravating smirk his beefy friend was displaying. Like a kid in the way of a runaway freight, Alvord sat there complacently grinning at death.

The crazy damn fool!

Berts tried to shout. His lungs felt as though they must burst through his ribs; and then when the words had thawed enough that he could move them he was scared to let them go. Alvord, still with that twisted grin on his mouth, was getting out of his chair and a distraction at this point could be just what Bill wanted.

He watched Alvord, straightening, empty his face of smoke, saw him stub out his butt on the top of the table a hand's breadth away from his untouched drink. He showed the calm of utter confidence and would have earned Matt's admiration could Berts have believed he was not stone blind. But who, having glimpsed that telltale sag, would be taking the Bud Hood boss so lightly?

Not Matt Berts, you could bank on that.

Still with his tolerant grin Alvord drawled, "Come outside with me, Billy. Got somethin' I want to say to you."

Carelessly turning, he threw open the door into Schweitzer's back yard and Cowboy Bill, scarce concealing his grim satisfaction, with the guile of a stalking cat tramped after him.

A chill rode down Matt Berts' crawling spine and threatened to shake the knees out from under him. The door banged shut. Frantic thoughts crammed his head and fear sawed through them like a dull-edged knife to jerk him onto his feet and root him there frozen, the futile and conspicuous target of all eyes.

He was petrified, scowling, when the crash of a gun made the lampflames jump.

In the deadlocked quiet someone near the bar cursed. The Bud Hood crew came en masse through the crowd with a high rebel yell, cuffing laggards aside, playing hell with the furniture. It was like old times—those times before Alvord and, secure in their beliefs, this bunch was preparing to paint the town red when that back door pulled open to frame the bulk of Burt Alvord. In cold scorn he confronted them above the dull shine of a smoking pistol.

"Bill won't be botherin' the cook for breakfast."

EIGHT

Cuidado, Hombre!

Burt Alvord had been in her thoughts many times since that kiss at the gate and the last sight she'd had of him impudently grinning from the shadows of the trail. In the turmoil of that moment she'd been glad to see him go, resenting his assumptions, hating and strangely frightened of the things he had roused in her. She tried to force her thinking away from channels she instinctively knew to be dangerous, but the demands of awakened hungers were not so easily put aside.

He was like no other man she had known. His half mocking, half humorously delving eyes had a way of suddenly filling with fire and she'd been witched by the excitement of what she'd glimpsed behind them. She'd caught a brashness there, a soul-shaking vision of the terrifying heights to which his untamed spirit could take her, and she was chafed with an intolerable restlessness that he should deliberately remain so long away.

Ten days and not one word—how dared he treat her in so cavalier a fashion! For the hundredth time she hastened to the window, peering through the cottonwoods' yellow-leaved branches toward a trail which maddeningly persisted in remaining empty. She had always thought of autumn as the graveyard of the seasons. Soon they'd have the winds again to remind them of encroaching winter. September was a bitter month. Especially when you were living off beef. The beef you had hoped to market.

She went into the bedroom and pulled off her dress. Her slip slithered into a heap on the floor, underthings flattening it. She was moving nakedly toward the closet when she caught the clop of hoof sound. Tensed with listening, a mounting excitement leaped into her eyes. She was crossing the room, hurrying into the office, when a mirror stopped her short.

Dashing back to the closet she got into a shirt. She wriggled into her Levi's, stamped on some boots. She pulled a jumper off the hook and was thrusting her shirt in as she sped to the window. But it wasn't Burt Alvord. It was only that fellow she'd caught sight of last week—Berts, Charlie'd called him.

She stood fists clenched, hard breathing, while he put up his horse. She watched him shake out a loop and go after another. She was waiting on the porch when he came riding by. Broad shouldered, clean shaven, clad in range clothes. He lifted his hat and turned when she called him. A cold-jawed man, bleak of eye, his look inscrutable.

He left the conversation up to her and after rummaging the slant of his cheeks Bella said, "I don't believe we've met before. Aren't you a friend of Burt Alvord's?"

"I've answered to worse things."

She looked at him curiously. "I've been expecting him down here."

He didn't seem to think that called for any answer.

"Are you helping Billy Stiles?"

"Well . . . no, ma'am. Not exactly."

"Did Kraitch—" She said carefully: "Why are you here?"

"To make sure no more of your cattle gets moved."

"But I thought Stiles—Where *is* Stiles?"

"I reckon he's in Willcox."

"Willcox! Does he imagine my cattle are being taken over there?"

"Couldn't say about that, ma'am."

"Can you say anything at all?"

Berts grinned. "I ain't plumb tongue tied."

"Then tell me why Alvord hasn't—"

"Told you, ma'am. I'm taking care of that."

"I don't see why he can't come down here himself—do you?"

"Well . . . yes. I expect he's kind of got his hands full right now. Had to ventilate a feller a couple of weeks back and the town don't seem to be settling down good to it."

Bella paled. "You mean he . . . killed some-body?"

Berts bit off a chaw and spat. "If he didn't the feller's got a rebate coming 'cause he sure as hell got planted."

Bella's thoughts went a little bit wabbly for a moment, but she couldn't help feeling if Burt were really in trouble the smart thing to do would be to come down here until it all blew over. She said as much but the man in the brush-clawed clothing shook his head.

"It ain't that kind of trouble, ma'am; it ain't the law that's hounding Burt. Guy pulled a gun and it was either shoot or grab a harp. Judge Page got a coroner's jury together and they had Burt cleared before midnight."

"Then I don't see—"

"It's the rowdy element's got their knives out for Burt. He's a marked man, ma'am. This bird that got killed was the Bud Hood foreman and the Bud Hood crew has swore to square it. Half the gamblers is back of them and the most of the cow crowd, not to mention the riffraff that don't like the way Burt's packing his tin. He couldn't slope now. He'd have to keep running the rest of his life."

Bella frowned at the man, hating this and despising it, impatient with the ridiculous views men stubbornly held about such matters. She wanted Burt here and there had ought to be some way. . . .

She said, "He can't expect to stand off the whole town."

"No, ma'am. He don't have to. There ain't no one hankering to lock horns with him; it's the cut-and-run breed he has to watch out for—the cold-deckers. He put it up to the Committee and they hired him Frank Aikens which is a pretty tough chicken. But all that done was drive them to cover. They're still out to git him.

"Burt rented him a shack on a flat west of town and just the other night, according to the way I heard it, a couple of guys made a try to get at him. He woke up too quick and drove them off. He found out next morning both of them was wearing high-heeled boots. He follered their sign to where they climbed on their horses, and give out that he knew them, thinking that might help. Mebbe it did; they ain't been back. But he's been shot at three times so a couple days ago the Committee hired another gent to help him. This guy's working under cover, pertending to hate Burt's guts—reason I know is I talked with him yesterday. He sees quite a heap of Burt's enemies and may get to hear something in time to pass the word."

"That could work both ways if they happened to get onto him."

"Not this guy. He's a gunsmoke galoot and he's

got plenty of connections. Stands in well with Dallas and the Bud Hood boys."

Bella winced at his mention of her brother. Dallas always had shown a tendency to wildness but she'd hoped he'd grow out of it. He was more weak than bad, a colt let run too long before bitting. A boy playing at badman, fooling himself with the crass delusion that by associating with men little better than outlaws he was proving himself a fellow to be reckoned with.

Sighing, Bella hauled her thoughts back to Alvord. Why did men have to be so damned stubborn? Pride was the source of all their troubles.

If she could just get him out here. . . . Charlie'd told her they needed Burt's guns on their side but it wasn't his guns she was thinking of now. "You can do something for me. Get hold of Alvord. Tell him something has come up and I must see him right away."

Berts shook his head. "He won't leave town till this is settled."

She looked up at him angrily. "He will if he knows I need him—"

"If you think that you better see him yourself. I've contracted to keep my eye on these cattle." Touching his hat Berts rode off.

Alvord was spending a lot of time these days hunkered down with a stick and his jackknife, whittling—studying out some new devilment was the way his enemies put it. This town was no Pearce and riding herd on a bunch of hard-drinking cowhands was proving a fulltime job.

He wasn't kidding himself. The cow crowd around here was riled and ugly. They were plainly watching for a chance to gang up on him. The whole sum and substance of conversation any more had to do with that killing and the way the bulk of these knotheads were carrying on you'd imagine that galoot hadn't had no more chance than a snowball in hell.

On his feet Cowboy Bill had been an over-bearing bully, blustery and quarrelsome, always packing a chip and expecting common waddies to get plumb out of his way. But now that he'd got what his actions had asked for this whole friggin country was out to clean his slate. Even those he'd used worst was running around like a conclave of gophers trying to get the sorry bastard fitted out with a halo.

You would think folks would have more goddam sense.

He turned it over some more and came up with the conviction there was too much smoke for the amount of fire kindled. All manner of forgotten things he had done were being dusted off and taken out for airing. There was an undertone of viciousness here he couldn't account for. He had never endeavored to make himself a stuffed shirt but the things he had done had just been done for the hell of it—not to pay off grudges or to better his condition. Way this bunch was talking a man would think, by grab, he was some kind of mad dog ready to snap or bite at anyone.

He felt confused and bewildered, unable to recognize himself in these rumors. If folks really believed he was that kind of critter it was sure as hell time he climbed onto high ground. Sure he'd moved a few cows but who in Christ's name hadn't? He'd run off a few Papago ponies too but he'd done it for a lark, not to make a business out of it. Now they were even telling it around that when he'd been a Border agent the only crooks he'd turned up were those with fat rewards on their scalps which wouldn't knuckle down to paying him off. They were saying that for a price he could be hired to do anything. They said he'd beat Bill out of that pacer and bragged that he had done it; that Bill had called him on it, daring him to draw, and that he'd been too yellow to put a hand near his gun; that on the night Bill had followed him into Schweitzer's back yard he'd shot him down without a chance—that the poor friendly cuss had gone out there unarmed.

One thing Burt saw plain as the horn on a saddle. There was a lot more to this than those Bud Hood boys were back of. Someone wanted him killed and in one hell of a hurry!

On account of Bar 6?

It was a possible assumption but not one Burt really favored. He found it hard to credit Bella's redheaded brother with a sufficient amount of savvy to have worked out any such method. Dallas wouldn't care to have his arrangements interfered with and might have learned through Stiles whom to blame for this setback. Billy Stiles didn't have any overload of judgment and, without at all meaning to put Burt in a jam, could have let it get out why he had climbed off their gravy train. He needn't have told Dallas personally; he might have let the word drop and someone else set it winging—one of those butchers who'd been slaughtering Charlie's cow-hands.

But even this didn't seem to fit like it belonged there. If the kid was hiring guns as well as a crew of rope-and-ring experts it would be more in keeping for him to sic them onto Alvord; and sure as hell someone had tried to catch his turkey those times they'd left tracks around his shack on the flats.

What was going on now was more like putting out poison. This whispering campaign was some-thing he couldn't strike back at; and all of a sudden Burt remembered Joel Kraitch.

There were a whole flock of reasons why Kraitch might be in back of this. The Crazy K owner was a spindling half-blind mouse of a man whom Alvord had long suspected of being neck deep in the hemp trade, and not as a fiber salesman. When he'd been working as a shadow man Burt had twice come within an ace of catching Kraitch at it but had never quite been able to get enough evidence. Nothing but Bar 6 lay between Kraitch's spread and the international line and, in view of what Burt suspected, it was a foregone conclusion Kraitch would like to get Bella out of there.

Burt reckoned he had better poke around that canyon. But he was a man who preferred to handle first things first, and what this burg mainly needed right now was a reminder that good health could prove a mighty transient asset.

With this notion prodding him he sent off a boy to round up some bottles. While the lad was away he stretched a rope across the street at an advantageous angle just outside Mr. Schweitzer's batwings. From this, at appropriate intervals, he hung five strings and when the boy returned Burt attached to the dangling ends of these an equal number of the longest necked bottles and stood off to admire his handiwork.

While he was waiting for the word to sift round he went into the saloon and cadged the loan of a cut-short pistol which he carelessly thrust into the waistband of his trousers. "Life insurance," he told Schweitzer, grinning.

Outside again he found quite a crowd assembled. Motioning the gathering off to one side he tightened the rope till that gleaming line of twirling glass stood at roughly seventeen hands above the road. "Nothin' up my sleeves," he smiled, and walked off forty feet.

He spun like a startled cat. All that could be seen of his draw was twin flashes. So swift and with such racket the crowd hardly grasped what was happening he emptied both guns in a thunder of concussions. With his left he broke strings while his right sent glass flying in forty directions, smashing the dropped bottles before they could touch ground. Ten rounds he unraveled in the space of five heartbeats and nothing but the neck of one splintered container was left hanging when he quit.

Dropping those smoking barrels in leather he flipped the borrowed pistol around by its trigger guard while he raked the crowd with a mocking stare. "Any of you jaw waggers craving to crash the pearly gates?"

That evening Burt Alvord rode out to the hog ranch to have a few words with the undercover man he'd talked the Vigilance Committee into hiring. A key thumper was picking out a tune on the ivories and Bill Downing had his frame propped against the mahogany with his red-veined nose looking redder than ever and Billy Stiles glumly nursing a shot glass beside him.

Alvord said to Stiles, "How you makin' it?" and

Stiles, looking irritable, growled, "Damn poorly."

He polished off his drink and Fat Emma, behind the bar, filled it up again, saying with her disapproving eyes on Alvord, "Tonight you can count your friends on one hand and you're doing my business no good by coming here. Why don't you get smart and turn in that damned tin?"

Alvord grinned. "Where's Annie?"

"Never you mind where she is. You keep away from her."

"This her idea?"

"Tell him," Fat Emma said to Downing and, when he kept his mouth shut, she said putting the flats of her hands on the bar, "Then I'll tell you myself. Either you stay away from her or she goes, one."

"Why?"

"Because she can't keep her mind on her business, that's why. All the time thinking of you, worrying about you, wondering why—"

"Hell, I can't help that."

"You can keep away from her—" She broke off, clamping her long lips tightly as a slim black-haired girl walked in from the back hall in a wrapper, saw Alvord and stopped with her whole expression suddenly changing. "Burt!"

"Hello, Annie," Burt grinned, ignoring Fat Emma's scowl. "Large evenin'?"

"It is now," the girl smiled, and led him back to her room.

• • •

The girl rolled over and sat up. "I've got to talk to you, Burt. Dallas Norton was here." Her anxious eyes searched his face. "Are you mixed up with Bar 6?"

"He think I am?"

"He was wild, Burt—awful. I never saw him like that, and it wasn't just the liquor. I'm afraid for you, honey. Honest—"

Burt grinned. "All's the matter with him his dad cut him off with fifty bucks an' he figures to get the rest back by stealin'. I've undertook to stop it."

She regarded him dubiously. "There's more to it than that. You didn't see him—he's crazy, Burt, gone off his rocker. You should have seen his eyes—the way he jerks and trembles. Whatever it is you've—"

"What did he say?"

"It wasn't so much what he said; it's the way he looked and acted. I got the feeling there was something big going on that he and you were both mixed up—"

"He mention any names?"

She shook her head. "Only you; he said you were going to be 'taken care of.' I think he was out of his head. Most of the time he kept talking about trains and—"

Burt, swinging round, caught hold of her roughly. "What's this about trains?" He was all

95

lawman now with a face hard as granite.

"I wasn't paying much attention. Something about trains and the Denver Mint—What's the matter? What are you doing?"

"Business, baby." Burt got off the bed and hustled into his clothes. "Here—" he dropped a handful of cartwheels on the bureau and grabbed his hat.

Back in Fat Emma's parlor he gave Stiles the nod and hurried out to the stable to pile the gear on his horse. Stiles showed up about the time he was getting finished and Burt said, "Downing pick up anything?"

"He's been tryin' hard enough. They've all clammed up."

"What have you got on Kraitch?"

"The hemp king?" Billy whistled. "Jeez—is he in on this?"

"I'm askin' you."

"First I ever heard of it. I was gettin' all my orders through Three-Fingered Jack. Never heard Kraitch mentioned."

"You wouldn't if I got this figured right; he ain't the kind to go tippin' his hand. He's usin' Dallas for cover but if Bar 6 goes up I'm bettin' Kraitch takes it over. Reason I called you out though is Dallas. That goddam fool's figurin' to stop the westbound."

Billy Stiles didn't laugh. He didn't seem too surprised. "Where'd you latch onto that?"

"He had a load on tonight. All he could talk about was trains."

"I'll string along up to there. Downing's been fillin' his ear for a week—all that crap he used to pull with Sam Bass. Kid lapped it up like black strap molasses, but that don't mean he'll try it. Where would he get the dope? Hell, he ain't got the guts."

"He's damn fool enough," Burt said. "I think he means to give it a whirl."

"We can sure as hell find out," Stiles said. "I'll get hold of Dunlap. About five dollars' worth will do it."

"Watch yourself," Alvord warned. "We don't want it gettin' back to him. Don't dig for any details—"

"I won't have to. Not with that guy. If there's anything in him it'll all come out."

NINE

The Turning Hour

Not many men in the West's factual history regularly packed two guns and were proficient with both. This traditional figure was mainly a creation of the late Ned Buntline and that ink-stained brigade who exploited his discovery. To this premise, however, there were notable exceptions; of these perhaps the greatest was Burt Alvord, a genius of dexterity, a wonderful rifle shot and sure death with pistols. This was no accident but the achievement of much practice. He burnt thousands of cartridges and despite his confident mien was not immune to worry.

He was worried now. Like most who follow a precarious livelihood he had a honed-sharp interest in small things. Blades of grass gave him their stories, lifted dust and sound of voices. He absorbed significance as a sponge stores water and, because of this faculty, he entertained some pretty uncomfortable thinking as he peered from the windows of his shack the next morning.

He was finally convinced that he'd become a marked man. All the carefree past was done with, put away like the bride's clothes after the wedding. Many of those he'd counted friends no longer spoke or even nodded and conversations, more often than not, showed an irritating habit of being forthwith suspended about as soon as he appeared. Eyes fled away from his and faces turned inscrutable whenever his glance fell across them. Unmistakable signs.

And there were others. Last night, hardly an hour after parting with Stiles, another attempt had been made to murder him. He'd been riding the pacer a couple of blocks west of Schweitzer's, making his rounds and thinking bitterly of Dallas, when a knife had come winking out of an alley, missing its goal by less than two inches. He had happened to lean back in a reach for the makings; this was all that had saved him.

The sun was up, it stood three hours high, when he rode into the pocket where he'd agreed to meet Billy. Stiles was already waiting. Bill Downing was with him.

"You was right," Stiles growled before he even got his horse stopped. "That damn kid means to go through with it—they're goin' to crack the flyer."

Alvord scowled. He put sharp eyes on Bill Downing.

The lanky Texican said, "Hell—don't blame me! All I done was spout off. I didn't suppose the fool would fall for it."

"You suggested this to him?"

" 'Course I didn't," Downing bridled. "I'd been

talkin' about some of them trains we stopped when I was flankin' Sam Bass, just augerin' like usual, passin' the time of day with the numbskull. When I seen the way his eyes was shinin'—"

"You figured you'd pull his leg a little?"

"Alls I said was what a waste of swell chances there wasn't nobody here with a mite o' real gumption. I never meant nothin' by it. The little punk was damn near droolin'. So I said Sam wouldn't of stood round pickin' his nose with that westbound flyer due to rip past on the eleventh totin' eighty thousand bucks in gold fresh outa the Denver mint."

While working for Wells Fargo Burt had been a frequent traveler on the run that carried this mintage. He knew from firsthand knowledge those details of procedure governing the handling of such shipments, even to the manner in which the railroad's safes were opened. These were closely guarded secrets imparted only to the trusted few who were committed to the actual management. Yet it did not occur to Burt until later to wonder how Fat Emma's night watchman had got onto the route and train involved.

He was too concerned with its impact on Dallas to be aware of the strangeness of that circumstance now. The glint of his eyes was like a curse as he sat his horse gloweringly inspecting the Texican. He had a fed-up look that made the cowboy, Stiles, step uneasily backward and away from Bill Downing, nor was this lost on the latter.

He growled in his throat but his guts couldn't stick it and he said in a whimpery nasal whine, "How the hell was I to know you wasn't goin' to like it? You pull Stiles off his payroll, you clamp down on his graft—I figured you was out to bust that kid. I thought you'd get a laff at him stickin' his neck out."

Alvord choked down his anger. This was neither the time nor the place for it. What was done was done. This whiskery hardcase couldn't be expected to understand how he was feeling about Dallas' sister.

Getting a grip on himself Alvord said, "I'm just buckin' him on them cattle. I wasn't aimin' to git his light snuffed or land the damn fool in Yuma. It's Kraitch I'm after, not that two-by-four kid."

"Kraitch!" Downing's brows jumped. Then a better shade of color climbed into his cheeks and he got up off his butt and mouthed another wad of twist. "I dunno about Kraitch, but if he's tied up with Dal—"

"Burt's got it figured Kraitch is usin' the kid."

"Usin' him for what?"

"Smokescreen, mostly," Alvord answered. "I think he'd like to get Bella Norton out of that canyon; less risk an' more handy for that hemp trade he's runnin'."

He scrubbed a hand across his jaw and considered Downing without seeing him. Strange thoughts were prowling around through his head and a dark foreboding choused a flock of cold shivers along the ridge of his spine. He wanted to whirl his horse and get out of the country; just ride and keep riding like he had as a kid when he'd took all he could of his old man's tantrums and envisioned a life of better tomorrows on the golden slopes of some far-distant hill. But he wasn't a kid any more and he knew putting hills between yourself and a tight spot seldom worked out to be the answer to anything. He was sure as hell going to have to stop Dallas someway. Bella'd never got over it if—

Downing's watching orbs had grown big as saucepans. He said, suddenly aghast: "You ain't cravin' to *stop* him?"

"I ain't cravin' to, no. But it looks like I'll have to."

They were both eyeing him now, as froze still and staring as though the sky had fell on them. Stiles growled, "Are you serious?"

Burt grinned without mirth. There was no use trying to explain it to these guys. He hadn't even got it worked out in his own mind; it didn't make sense that he should risk his neck for a no-account skunk that would gun him down like a snake if the chance come. All Burt could think of was Bella—of how she'd be feeling if this antigodlin numbskull got his neck in a sling. "You know how to get hold of him?"

Stiles shook his head. "He's pretty damn slick at keeping himself out of sight. How're you figurin' to stop him?"

"Thought if I could reach him I might scare—"

"Won't work," declared Downing. "You won't get the job done that way. Kid's too damn stubborn."

"Well . . . I could hogtie the—"

"Thing to do is ketch him at it. Wait'll he starts to swing up an' then grab him. That way," Downing said, "you got a club to hold over him."

Burt scowled awhile, but that seemed like the best bet. He slanched a moody look at Stiles. "You know where they're going to pull this?"

Stiles shrugged. "Suppose I coulda found out but you—"

"Bound to be this side of Cochise," Downing grumbled. "Near the top of the grade where they'll be puffin' an' pantin'—only place *to* pull it. Goddam halfwit would savvy that."

He spat and wiped his handlebars. "Kind of feel like in a way this whole deal is my fault. If I hadn't been shootin' off my mouth he wouldn't of latched onto this damfool notion. I'll devote a little time to helpin' you, Burt."

"Thanks," Alvord said. "Expect I'll need all the help I can get."

Stiles, suddenly grinning, slapped a hand to his

thigh. "Got it," he chortled—"by God I got it! I know just how to work this. I spent two months of ridin' with them pelicans on that cow job. I'll tell Dunlap this deal looks good to me, that I wanta be cut back into the cavvy."

Downing studied Alvord while Burt thought this over.

"Be a cinch," Stiles said eagerly. "They've got to have dynamite. I can slip back into the mountains and lift all they'll need from one of the mines. Jack knows I've worked with powder; he'll be glad of the help I can give 'em. What do you say? Be just like knockin' off ducks with a slingshot. I'll keep in touch. You fellers can be ready to jump in when the fun starts."

Burt didn't like it. Seemed like to him Stiles was taking all the risk; but he couldn't think of anything better. He chucked a look at Downing. "What do you think, Bill?"

"Sounds fair enough," Downing nodded. "Was we dealin' with guys which had heard the owl hoot I'd be inclined to say it was a little mite desprit. But this Dunlap don't know dung from wild honey. And Billy's worked with him before—I don't reckon they'll get their hackles up."

"You keep your eyes skinned," Burt cautioned as Stiles went over to his horse and jerked the girths taut. "One slip an' those skunks'll make a colander of you."

TEN

Prelude to Action

Riding the rimrocks above Guadalupe Canyon Matt Berts rested the Winchester across the prong of his square-skirted saddle and wondered how much longer Bella Norton could hold out.

In the fifteen nights he'd been prowling this range he had come to understand the girl was troubled by more than rustlers. Nor was he lulled into imagining she had seen the last of those. They were quiet now, cunningly hidden, but this didn't have to mean they had been scared off.

He'd been curious about Alvord's interest, Burt never having much been bothered about other people's problems. But these weren't just anyone's problems and now, having met the owner, Matt could understand his friend taking a hand. A whole galaxy of women had passed through Burt's arms but no one like Bella Norton. She'd be something from another world to a roughneck of Alvord's character; would have exerted a tremendous attraction.

Matt poked his thoughts around for a bit and, cautiously turning them over, came up with the reluctant conviction she had about reached the end of her rope.

She might have sweated this out with a backlog of cash but he had found it increasingly evident Bar 6 had no cash reserves to fall back on. Witness Charlie combing the brush with a crew of four punchers where in this kind of country ten would have hardly been any too many. For the best part of two weeks now all five had been at it, trying to push enough of the old stuff out of these rocks to make a shipment.

When he'd told the girl's ramrod this was asking for trouble Charlie'd sleeved off his face and inquired what he reckoned he was being kept around for. His hands were too beat out for much grumbling but Matt had picked up enough to be reasonably sure they hadn't pocketed one cent in wages since Old Man Norton had kicked the bucket. They were making this gather out of sheerest necessity and, somewhere back in the brush, Dallas' bunch would be licking their chops and getting a laugh at this picture of Charlie doing all the hard work.

He wondered if Alvord had any suspicion of how bad things actually were with this outfit. Likely not, he decided. Burt had only spent a day here and most of that time probably thinking of the girl. You couldn't blame him for that. Matt couldn't, anyway.

Staring down through the deepening dusk to where the glow of the fire threw out its pinpoint of claret, he wondered if the herd Charlie's boys down there were holding had reached sufficient proportions to fetch Dallas out of hiding. Must be three hundred head in the gather by this time.

Matt's brother was a cattleman with a ranch over near Willcox and it made him grit his teeth to think of all the hours of grueling, joint-straining, dangerous toil Charlie's bunch of bronc cattle represented. Working wild ones off these rocky slopes was no job for a greenhorn. One of the boys had his back bruised from hip to shoulder but he had stayed right in there riding with the rest.

Though he'd had no chance after taking this job to get in any private talk with Stiles, he'd been told by one of the Bar 6 hands it was the opinion of the outfit there must be six or eight guys engaged in Dallas' stealing. At least one of these gents, by Matt's personal estimate, was apt to be considerable careless with his shooting iron. While this didn't particularly prey on Matt's mind, it resolved him to feel no compunction should he ever find one of those whoppyjawed chipmunks peering up the tube of his rifle.

As soon as the shadows got thick enough to hide him, Berts changed position, stopping his mount beside a patch of squatting cedar partway down the canyon's wall. He chose this spot because it offered a straight and unimpeded run to both the canyon floor and the rim he'd just come off of and, if he had to move at all, he wanted to be able to move in a hurry.

He wasn't especially expecting tonight would be any different from the previous nights but with a shorthorn like Dallas it didn't pay to relax a wrinkle. A snatch of three hundred steers could show a sizable profit in any rustler's books.

The moon was in the last quarter. It wouldn't be throwing much light and this fact might coax Dallas into striking. He could ask all right for a bigger herd but he couldn't well expect to find a better place to grab one. They were bedded on the canyon floor a quarter mile north of where the cook's fire showed its red spark of light. All Bella's brother would need to do was create an uproar and they wouldn't quit running this side of the line.

Charlie, Matt thought, must have had the same notion for he'd camped the chuck wagon south of the cattle; and that was where the crew lay. Only one man had been told off to ride circle. By the usual procedure they'd been doing this in relays and, during the earlier stages of the gather, Bella's ramrod had kept two men at it constant; but as the cattle became accustomed to being held and a little of the wildness wore off the larger number Charlie'd rotated the hands in one-man shifts.

Shortly before he had climbed to his vigil Matt had got the boss aside to protest this new arrangement, half expecting the old man to rear back on his haunches. Weariness overrode the resentment in Charlie's voice. "The boys have got to have some rest. If they don't we're going to lose the damn brutes anyway."

Time dragged. The moon's red sickle dropped lower.

A cowbell's broken clanking drifted out of the south and Matt's atrophied faculties listened to its murmur for three full seconds before shock jerked his face around. *What the hell was a cowbell doing down there!*

He was tense in the saddle, still staring, when sound avalanched from up-canyon with the racket of hell emigrating on cart wheels. Streaks of light crisscrossed through the uproar. Out of the blackness below him a bull bawled alarm and Matt heard the cattle get onto their feet.

It was at about this time that Burt Alvord, detained beyond intention, wove his horse through the brush and rode into the rendezvous. Both men sat waiting for him beside a guarded fire.

"Duck soup," Stiles said, chuckling, as Burt got out of leather. "Dunlap was ready to kill the fatted calf—took it down whole. I'm to furnish the powder. Jack'll take care of the engine crew. Dallas is goin' to handle the express car and I'm to blow the safes. God, what prize ninnies! Just

111

the pair of them's all there is in on it. But we're bigger dopes than they are."

"How you mean?"

"They aim to stop that train right outside Cochise. It's the top of the grade; she won't be movin' no faster than a cow with burnt feet. Why, they—"

Alvord's deep voice cut in. "Elucidate dopes."

"What else could you call us? Here we go to all this work to keep a couple dumb bastards from makin' fools of theirselfs. Why not let 'em *be* fools?"

"Mebbe," Alvord said, "you better ride that trail again."

"Christ, it's simple enough. Let 'em go ahead and stop the train. Let 'em cut off the coaches and take the express car down the track. Lemme crack them safes accordin' to schedule, then you boys step in and take over the dough."

Alvord eyed him. "You gone off your rocker?"

"You're the one that oughta get his head looked at!" Stiles flared, cheeks darkening. "Eighty thousand bucks—Jesus Christ! Where else can you get that kinda dough just by reachin' your hand out?"

"I ain't reachin' it out," Alvord said— "An' you ain't, either. I'm surprised at you, Billy."

"Billy's right," Downing grunted. "It's the chance of a lifetime. Let them yaps get it ready then we'll step in an' grab it—"

"What you'd be grabbin' is a long sweat at Yuma. Get your eyes open, chum. You ain't talkin' about Texas."

"Ain't that what I'm tellin' you? In Texas they got Texas Rangers. Here all you got's a couple half-baked sheriffs that couldn't find hair on a dog."

"And what do you reckon that Denver mint and this Southern Pacific is going to be doin'?"

Downing sneered. "Sounds like your guts is about to shrivel away to fiddle strings."

Alvord stared through a tightening stillness until the lanky ex-Texican found something else to put his eyes on. Then he said, "Be a good time to drop that talk right now. We ain't about to rob no express cars."

Next day about noon Alvord unlatched the gate and rode into Bar 6 headquarters. The place looked deserted but that was as it should be since he'd reckoned his arrival to catch Bella alone. Swinging off before the house he stepped onto the porch and thumped four knuckles against the wood of the door. He expected she would probably be a little mite surprised.

He'd gone to considerable effort slicking up for this occasion, having brushed off the visible parts of his boots, slapped dust from his trousers and reluctantly parted with a pocketload of cash for the ten-gallon Stetson which was covering his baldness. Burt had always been touchy about his lack of top hair.

He stood around for awhile to give her time if she were changing, then clouted the door again. When still nothing happened he raised his voice in a shout.

He was never able later to figure why he stepped into the house but the next thing he knew he was in it, leaning above Dave Norton's desk, laboriously deciphering the contents of a twice-creased sheet of blue-lined paper.

My dear Miss Norton, *the message read,* it is with extreme reluctance that I take my pen in hand. Being cognizant of my true feelings you will understand my embarrassment. Unfortunately recent events make it imperative your father's note of hand, which I've been holding this past twelvemonth, be redeemed at the earliest possible. Because of the esteem in which I held him, as well as to lighten your load during that time of grief, I did not push this claim against his estate. Only the most pressing demands of unfulfilled obligations have forced me to call this matter to your attention. If there were another way out, even now I should be glad to consider it; if the debt has not been satisfied by the seventeenth of this month I shall have to ask for an accounting, distressing though such a course would be. Your brother's depredations leave me no alternative. If you have the cash available or can make a suitable arrangement, I suggest you get in touch with me in advance of the time above mentioned.

It was signed J. S. Kraitch and was dated September 2.

The sound of approaching horses finally pulled Alvord's eyes from the paper. Stepping onto the porch he saw the distant shapes of two horsebackers approaching the place from down-canyon. The nearer of these looked a lot like Matt Berts; he appeared to be supporting the other man in his saddle. A gusty wind was whipping up the grit, making it hard for Alvord to see well; the pair were quite near before he recognized old Charlie in the slumped figure Matt was steadying.

Alvord was waiting at the gate when they reached it. There was a blood-stained bandage underneath the torn shirt and Charlie's cheeks looked the color of damp wood ash. His eyes were open but he wasn't seeing much. "Rustlers," Matt said. "Help me get him into the house—Bella said I was to put him to bed and fetch a doc out."

"Take that piller out from under him," Alvord

said when they'd shucked the old man of torn shirt and clawed Levi's and got him stretched out in the brass-knobbed bed formerly used by Bella's dad. "Shove it in here on the springs when I ketch up the mattress—that's it. He's sufferin' mostly from shock and the loss of blood it looks like. Main thing's to raise his feet and see that he's kept warm. I don't think we better bother that rag. Get his boots pulled off while I dig up some blankets."

When this had been managed Berts, tagging him out to the porch, said abruptly: "I better get poundin'. I got—"

"Another five minutes ain't goin' to make much difference. Let's have the story."

So Berts told how Charlie had been trying to scrape up enough old stuff to ship. "Had about three hundred bedded down in that gather. It was darker than hell with the blower off when this bunch comes skally-hootin' out of the blackness; boys done their best but nothin' on earth coulda held them critters. I guess we saved about eighty, not countin' the cripples. Rest of them's scattered—"

"Was it Dallas?" Burt asked.

"That's what everybody figures. I can tell you this much: there won't be no cattle shipped off this spread before spring. Take 'em two months at least to get another herd together. Couple of the boys got roughed pretty bad. You seen what happened to Charlie. We shared the tough luck around though; we got three of them monkeys."

He rasped his jaw and looked thoughtful. "Funny thing about that. One chunk of this buzzard bait was workin' for Kraitch. Remember that buck-toothed waddy they had reppin' at Two Diamond? Slug caught him straight on and tore the back of his head off."

ELEVEN

West Coast Express

Court was in session at Tombstone and Matt Berts, as he threw a leg over his saddle to go after the sawbones Bella had ordered, was cherishing the prospect of indulging himself with a holiday. Be like old times the way that town would be crowded. All the high rollers, fancy women and tent shows would be out in full force and if a man couldn't pick up a few bucks in that company he could at least cut the dust and catch up on his auguring.

"Guess I'll ride along with you," Alvord abruptly decided. "I've got to appear in a case that's set for tomorrow and there don't seem much use in my hangin' around here."

"Glad to have you," Matt said, thinking to exercise his talking talents, but he was soon disabused of that notion. Alvord set the pace and it was not conducive to protracted conversation. When they slowed to breathe the horses he seemed lost in his thinking and, as often as not, never answered Matt at all.

Berts finally shut up to do some thinking of his own. But when they came in sight of the Courthouse steeple and the hoists of the Vizna and Lucky Cuss shafts Alvord slowed to a walk and, getting out the makings, settled back on the leather. "Did it seem like to you that bunch was after those cattle?"

Berts looked at him, surprised. "I wouldn't have said they rode over to borry no chunk of fire."

"All the times before they've tried to keep their visits quiet—"

"You know any way to keep a stampede quiet?"

Alvord shook his head, and then: "It's uncommon odd. Up to now they've been satisfied to keep their operations in the cut-an'-run class—"

"They had to do the work themselves. They never had no chance to get away with a gathered herd."

"It ain't just that; all the way through this deal is different. All the risk before has been with Bar 6. This was bold and open; they had to come right out and swap lead with you fellers."

Berts' eyes narrowed. "You're thinkin' maybe it wasn't Dallas?"

"I'm thinkin' the reason back of it was different. It keeps trampin' my mind the main object last night was to break up that gather."

They rode the next several lengths in silence. Then Matt asked abruptly, "This goin' to make any changes in that job you give me to handle? You wanta call me off?"

"You don't figure that bunch will be back right away do you?"

"More like to hole up and lick their wounds for a spell—they didn't get out of that too damn cheap. But they'll be back, all right; no use figurin' they won't. They got that spread on a hard place. Couple of more pushes an' it'll go down like a stack of wood."

They turned into Allen and Matt, studying Alvord, found it hard to remember when he'd last seen Burt smile. Wasn't much fun to be around him any more. All the humor seemed to have been scoured out of his system and the change, Berts reflected, dated back to the day they'd made him marshal of Willcox. There were dark spots under his eyes now, deeper lines graven round his nostrils. He had the honed-down look of a hungry hound.

"How you and that cow crowd makin' it?" Matt asked.

Alvord brushed that aside. "They've gone under cover. Suppose you let that rustler-chasin' go for a spell. I'll be hung up here two-three days more than likely. Might find somethin' you could do if you want to stick around."

"Suits me."

"Fixed all right for cash, are you?"

"I wouldn't turn down more," Matt grinned.

"Somethin' coming up I might could use another hand on." Burt twisted his head, peering

121

at him, still with that considering frown on his cheeks. "You be satisfied to make three hundred for a couple of hours work?"

"Damned if I wouldn't," Matt chuckled. He cuffed the horn of his saddle. This was more like the Burt he had used to run around with. "What bank we fixin' to bust?" he said, grinning.

"No bank," Alvord scowled, "but it could be just as risky. Young Norton's got it in his mind to stop the westbound flyer."

Berts' jaw dropped. He finally pulled his face together and displayed a kind of parched grin. "You're slippin', pal. You used to do better—"

"This ain't no goddam joke," Alvord growled. "I happen to know the kid means to go through with it."

Very quietly Berts whistled. "And you're goin' to help him?"

"I been figurin' to stop him."

Never had Matt seen his friend look so grim, so indescribably bitter. "And what must I do?" he said finally.

"Mebbe you better keep out of this—"

"And pass up that three hundred dollars?" Berts snorted. "I'd have to work a long while to make that much mazuma."

"All right," Alvord shrugged. "Send your pill-roller out to see Charlie. Then get yourself a fresh horse and fetch Stiles and Bill Downing.

I want the three of you back of King's saloon by eleven o'clock tomorrow night."

Five minutes short of the appointed hour Burt Alvord, with both guns riding the swell of his thighs, swung north up Fourth past the silent black shell of the abandoned Can Can, turned west on Fremont, passed the lamp lighted windows of the City Hall, cut obliquely south and through the noisy gloom reached the hard-packed ground of King's rear premises. The saloon, by the sounds, was doing about all the business the housemen could handle and the Frenchman was dealing faro.

Three shapes drifted out of the dark and, after making sure he was with the right three, Alvord chose a spot some thirty feet from the toilet and asked Stiles if there were anything new to report.

"I got the dynamite," Stiles answered, belligerently adding—"an' some canvas sacks."

When the lack of conversation got a little uncomfortable Downing took a hand, saying, "Look at this thing reasonable, Burt. You're puttin' a hell of a strain on the bonds of friendship—"

"Way I recall it you offered your help."

"Sure," Stiles said. "Sure he did—same as me." His voice came panting through the rasps of his breathing, spilling out in a goaded snarl of desperation. "What the hell you reckon we are—

complete idjots? I let you talk me outa one good thing . . ." A raging sense of defeat unsettled him, and he cried: "Damned if I'm goin' to let you do it again!"

Downing's persuasive tones filled the breach. "Look at it this way. Say we let that train get stopped. We nab the kid before he does any damage but the alarm goes out. Gold might even turn up to be missin'. Anyhow we've stuck our necks out an' all the tongue-oil in Texas won't—"

"All right," Alvord said, "I reckon you'll do it in spite of hell or high water. If there's anyone against this damned thing besides me, let him say so."

Matt Berts kind of sighed. It gave the only competition to the sounds pouring out of the saloon's open windows.

"I guess," Alvord said on a note of grim finality, "the Southern Pacific's due to call off some dividends. Who's goin' to boss it?"

"You know the ropes," Stiles grunted. "Give your orders."

"We'll need complete changes of clothing; I'll leave that up to Downing. We'll pick up some horses on the edge of town. For a cover we'll use that back room at Schweitzer's, start a poker game there an' make a deal with the swamper. Downing'll have the new clothes waitin' an' when we've got the deal set up we'll put on these duds and, while we're hittin' a lope for Cochise, Bill will pick up our own things an' have 'em waiting for us to get into at the old adobe.

"Now I'll take care of the alibi. Stiles, with his sacks an' powder, will join Jack an' Dallas just before they jump the train. Berts will see to the broncs, hustle back an' cover Dallas and those boys in the engine an' ride herd on 'em till I swing up to take over. Stiles will take care of Dunlap an' cut the coaches loose. I'll be holdin' the crowd back. When we're ready to roll me an' Stiles will hop on. Soon's we've got that car where we want it I'll take over the cab an' Billy an' Matt will go to work on the express car. When they've got the gold sacked we'll make for the horses, Berts packin' the loot an' me an' Stiles keepin' tabs on Dallas an' Dunlap. We leave the broncs where we found 'em, leave the loot with Downing along with the duds, get into our own clothes, climb back into Schweitzer's an' be just about ready to pass out with surprise when someone busts in to tell us what's happened."

Matt Berts let go of a stifled guffaw. Downing scowled.

Alvord said, "Any questions?"

Stiles wanted to know what they'd do with the prisoners.

"Turn 'em loose in the sandhills."

"They'll be hotter'n a blister!"

"So they'll be hot. What of it? They won't be knowin' who we are with scarfs up an' strange clothin'. All you got to do is keep your damn mouths shut—what's eatin' on you, Bill?"

"What's the matter with lettin' me—"

"I've give you a job."

"Kid stuff!" Downing snorted. "I've had more damn experience—"

"An' blown it all over town. Even spillin' your guts to Dallas—which he'll damn well remember. Use your head."

Downing continued to grumble. He was a fiery quick-tempered rooster, a man who liked to feel his weight, rather vain of his reputation as one of this locality's toughest customers; and he had a Southern Gentleman complex regarding anything touching his "honor." He made it very vociferously obvious he considered himself sold short in this deal.

Berts interrupted to ask the exact date and time of the project.

"Night of the eleventh." Alvord blew out his cheeks. "We'll gather at Schweitzer's an' get the game goin' early. Allow an hour for the ride. Train crests the grade at eleven ten—"

"By God, Burt," Downing cut in with his plaint again, "you can say what you like but it stands to reason that a man who has ridden stirrup to stirrup with Sam Bass—"

"Jesus H. Christ!" Alvord's tone was fed up

126

with it. "Go ahead! Take my place an' shut up about it! I'll tend the clothes an' the goddam horses!"

Cochise Station was a stove and a key in a two-by-four shack painted an off-shade known as "railroad yellow" and set down in the desert ten miles west of Willcox. That was a pretty tough grade from Willcox to Cochise and the heavily-laden westbound flyer was ten minutes late when it came groaning and puffing into sight of the wigwag.

This was the Express, the line's pride and joy, not doing hardly better than ten miles per hour when her engine breasted the yellow-painted box and the telegraph operator popped his tousled head out, considerably surprised and even more bewildered to see the shapes of two men run up out of the dark, swing aboard the crack train just ahead of the combination money-and-baggage car and start clambering toward the locomotive.

The key-pounder swung half around to peer after them, forgetful of stiff neck and cold desert wind, in the amazed curiosity aroused by this occurrence. What kind of a graft were those bindle stiffs working?

His ears were filled with the whine of the wind, the engine's chug-chug-chugging, the continuous clatter of wheels on the rail joints. He couldn't see the men now. With the last of the pullmans about to clickety-clack past he was knuckling his eyes, beginning to wonder by God if he were having hallucinations, when there was a monstrous clanking of drawbars and drivers as slack crashed out of the couplings and the engine was hidden behind a cloud of white steam.

"Goddlemighty!" he gasped. "The hoghead's big-holed it!"

The crack flyer was stopped, no doubt about that—and stopped where it hadn't any business stopping either. He flung an agonized glance at the semaphore but it was straight up and down; he hadn't made any blunder. He ran out onto the platform and was about to jump down when a husky voice came at him out of the blackness: "Expect we can handle this without your help."

His startled eyes found the man, a tall rawboned fellow with something tied across his face and a long-barreled pistol carelessly dangling from one hand. And he gulped, understanding.

The express car doors skreaked open, yellow lamplight flooding out onto the cinders; and he saw Dare, the messenger, putting his head out, and the upper part of another man showing in the light, gruffly advising Dare to "Come down outa that!" and the fellow near the platform motioning Dare to come away.

The operator's knees were shaking but, when he saw two of the bandits duck between the opened car and the long line of darkened coaches, he had enough presence of mind to yell: "For Christ's sake set the hand brakes!"

A conductor and several brakemen, all swinging lanterns, were now making toward the front of the train and a number of the aroused and more inquisitive passengers were commencing to put in a rather garrulous appearance. The man who'd spoken to the operator came hurrying out of the night's windy shadows to turn these back, his big pistol glinting wickedly in the light of the train crew's lanterns.

One of the pair who'd uncoupled the coaches threw out a quick yell and the man with the gun trailed him back toward the engine. The operator, suddenly coming to life, dashed into his shack and started pounding the key.

About a mile down the track, when they'd got close to the horses, the man with the gun ordered the hoghead to stop. The other pair of bandits climbed out of the cab and a few minutes later there was a hell of an explosion from the car behind the tender and a roundabout clatter of falling debris. Lazily shifting his weight the masked gun-packer drawled, "I'm advisin' you gents to hold this here iron horse of your'n right where she squats for the next ten minutes. I don't aim to have to waste any cartridges on you bucks."

He gave them a curt nod and dropped to the

ground. They listened to his big-roweled spurs and to the crunch of his boots fading out across the gravel. The fireman spat on his hands and picked up his shovel but the man behind the throttle squeaked a frantic protest. "What's the matter with you, bub? Didn't you see that guy's eyes?"

Downing waited till Berts had got the money secured, then swung into his saddle and, taking the lead, began pushing the horses for all they were worth. Willcox lay east and Stiles was sure they were headed south but he didn't want any argument with a boss of Bill Downing's caliber— the guy was a heap too apt to reach for his pistol. He could get damn ugly when things didn't suit him.

They had picked up these broomtails on Alvord's advice from the bunch staked and hobbled along the town's outskirts every night by squatters and freighters, collecting saddles and bridles from the place where Alvord's fore-thought had cached them. That was one thing you sure had to say for Burt Alvord—he had a head on his shoulders and a keen eye for detail.

They were pounding across a dry lake now, filling the night with the clamor hoof-drummed off its flintlike surface. Stiles became prey to an uncomfortable worry this racket might fetch pursuit spurring after them. But just as he was about to put the fear into words, Downing swung east and in almost no time Stiles picked out the lone adobe looming gaunt against the scattering of lights flung up by Willcox, two miles distant.

As they rode up to the place Alvord rushed out to meet them with the clothes left at Schweitzer's. While they were changing Burt unsaddled the barefoot horses and, with a slap on their rumps, sent them flying across the flats. Admonishing them to hurry, he got the discarded clothes and gear out of sight; everything they weren't going to wear he took away someplace. And then he hustled them townwards while Downing bragged what a cinch it had been. "Just like guttin' a slut," the Texan chuckled.

Alvord asked abruptly: "How'd you make out with Dunlap an' Dallas?" and there was a moment of strained silence wherein nothing was heard but the rasp of their bootsteps.

Berts was the first to get out his story. "I was keepin' my peepers on that pair in the engine, never figurin' the kid would have the guts to make a break. I had to get a little rough with that clown of a coal-shoveler and whiles I was doing it the kid made a dive out the righthand winder." He said uncomfortably, "I coulda shot him, of course, but didn't reckon you'd think well of it. So I let the damn punk go."

Alvord made no comment. "What about Dunlap?" He swung his head toward Stiles.

"I done what I had to," Stiles growled irritably. "When you was layin' this out, none of us remembered Jack was goin' to be knowin' me. Never thought of it myself till I come to put the gun on him. We was workin' on that couplin' . . . I could see them bars at Yuma closin' round me. I banged him over the head with my gun. He never knew what hit him."

He kind of wished he could see the look on Burt's face but there wasn't any moon and the goddam stars didn't help much reading expressions. Like before Burt was keeping his thoughts to himself. Stiles couldn't get rid of the feeling though that Alvord was kind of put out about Dunlap; and he was almighty right.

After another five minutes of clatter from Downing, Burt swung back to the subject. "What'd you do with the body?"

"Dragged it over in that brush off north of the tracks."

"You pull the wipe off his mug?"

"You think I look like a idjot?"

Alvord didn't say what he thought Billy looked like, and this gravelled Stiles more, unaccountably disquieting him. He didn't understand this grouchy moodiness of Alvord's nor care for the increasing reticence Burt showed them. As with most ignorant people, what he couldn't understand Stiles distrusted. By the time they got into the back yard at Schweitzer's he'd begun to wish he hadn't let Burt talk him into this.

It wasn't until several hours later it occurred to him with a shock of cold fear and astonishment that in their excitement and haste to get back to the card table they'd none of them noticed what Burt had done with the gold.

TWELVE

Exhibition of Talent

At Bar 6 that night before it got dark old Charlie, out of bed but still chair-ridden and just about ready to climb through his hat, was grumbling to Bella he'd as soon die of lead poisoning "as be took off with the creepin jitters" when they heard the wagon roll into the yard. Charlie cocked an ear. That would be Puddin Taylor, on the ranch books as cook, who'd been off scouring town trying to find enough credit for another load of staples—and not the kind you drove in no fencepost. Now at least they'd have news, something to jaw about maybe.

Taylor was a wiry redheaded sixfooter with a limp he'd acquired some eight or nine years ago when an outlaw bronc had smashed him into the fence. He'd got the handle hung on him from his everlasting habit of "boggin a few raisins down in dough and calling her puddin."

Dumping a bundle of mail into the ramrod's lap he limped over to where Bella was working at the stove, lifted the lid off a pot, had a sniff and snapped testily, "You're goin' to ruin the old fool's pilot with that kinda fofaraw—you want a gut and some horns for it?"

135

Before Bella could answer, Charlie let out a roar like a prodded bull. "Puddin, you hairy-brained misfit, start unloadin' the news before I snatch a leg off this table an' clout you!"

The cook turned a face of injured innocence. "News? Oh—you mean about the Cochise Hardware an' Tradin' Company gettin' in them John Deere—All right, all right! Keep the plug in your bottle. Chacon's come back—"

"Augustin Chacon! *Paludo?*"

"No less," Taylor grinned. "Whole cussed town of Tombstone's buzzin' with it—you never seen such a boltin' of doors an' winders! Eight complete families has dug for the tules an' half of what's left expected to go any minute. Lord Gawd, what a uproar—town's got more excitement than a rat-tailed bronc tied short in fly time. Sheriff's swore in ever' able-bodied guy up to ninety an' they was barricadin'—"

"But what's he *done?*" demanded Charlie.

"Ain't done nothin'—yet. It's what he might be *goin'* to do that's got 'em all runnin' round in circles. Someone seen his bunch Injunin' along through the hills just west of the Grand Central. Personal," Puddin said skeptically, "I don't believe the old vinegarroon's within two hundred mile of this country."

After the cook had gone out to get his wagon unloaded Bella said, "Do you suppose we ought to take some precautions? I—"

136

Charlie snorted. "What kinda precautions can you take against that guy? But I don't reckon we need to worry; ain't nothin' around Bar 6 that would be like to take his fancy. That *ladino*'s huntin' bones that's still got plenty of meat on."

Just the same old Charlie was more uneasy than he was admitting. Augustin Chacon was no kind to yell boo at or idly dismiss with any shrug of the shoulders. He was in many respects typical of Mexican bandits, robbers of the rich and protectors of the poor; but in several important particulars he held a niche not shared by anyone else. He was, for one thing, the most notorious bandit in the entire Southwest, a *bandido puro* on whose scalp there was a fortune in bounty money.

Tall, gaunt and powerful he had a lot of Indian blood in his veins—definitely not Papago. He hid his black-browed face behind a mass of bushy never-trimmed whiskers and was a butcher who killed for the sheer love of agony, the sadistic pleasure of watching men writhe.

He had a hideout somewhere in the Sierra Madre Mountains from which it was his custom to steal across the line in the very dead of night, plundering at will and killing all who opposed him. And he had gotten away with so many of these raids he was by now considered in the nature of an institution, even though a very bad one.

His especial preference was for isolated

settlements and mining camps and the meat he liked best was that of deputy sheriffs. He was utterly merciless, completely terrible, credited already with the murders of upwards of eighty persons and, by actual count, twenty-five of these Americans. Nor did he confine his activities to night forays or to that country most adjacent to the border. He had carried his ravaging as far north as Morenci, Clifton and the outskirts of Phoenix. He was the boldest, baddest, most feared and hated outlaw of his time.

All these things old Charlie knew; they were common property and not to be denied. He had himself observed the knife work on one of *Paludo*'s victims, and he could still get the shakes just thinking about it. If Chacon came to Bar 6 there was nothing they could do but try to die bravely.

Hoping to chouse Bella's thinking into trails less harrowing he said, speaking at random, "Wasn't that Alvord's bull fiddle voice I heard the other night?"

Bella nodded. "He was around for awhile; he didn't stay long."

"Same night the doc was here?"

"Yes. Charlie, do you suppose Chacon—"

"There you go! Every time I fetch that feller's name into the jawin' you ack like a sick calf or go to diggin' up somethin' else to make talk with. An' never mind stirrin' all that clatter with your cookin'. If he was back here again—"

"Again!" Bella, wheeling away from the stove, looked surprised. "You mean to say Burt Alvord was here that same day *earlier?*"

"Helped Matt Berts load me into that bed."

"Then he probably never lef—"

"I heard the pair of 'em ride off."

"But why in the world would he decide to come back—"

"What I'm wonderin' myself." Charlie peered at her, thoughtful. "You an' him makin' sheeps eyes?"

"That's absurd!"

She didn't rightly look it; not with all that color showing.

The Bar 6 ramrod did some silent swearing. That she should become seriously interested in Alvord was the last thing Charlie'd ever imagined—or wanted. Not that Burt wasn't all right. In his way Burt Alvord was a feller to tie to; but his way wasn't anything you'd want in your livingroom or for a girl like Bella to get herself hitched up with.

Here he'd thought all the time the way she'd been moping round was on account of that money her dad had borrowed from Kraitch. Enough to make anyone start grabbing leather to get beat over the head with a demand for that much money; but you couldn't blame Kraitch. He had his problems, too, and none but a mighty good friend to Bar 6 would have held off this long with Dallas busting a gut to put the spread on the skids.

Charlie shook his head. If she had to go getting romantical notions why the hell didn't she twine them around someone like Kraitch and not a gun toting roughneck who couldn't spell his own name!

Women—hell's fire!

And then Bella was saying, "He wanted to know how we were fixed; how much longer we could hang on if he didn't get Dallas stopped."

The old man felt like snorting. Alvord's motives, to him, weren't no harder to see through than a fresh scrubbed window. Burt wasn't the kind to ride clean back here from town to be asking fool questions that didn't concern him no way. Nothing but an excuse so's he could honeyfogle round—

"You should have seen his face when I told him about that twenty thousand dollars the ranch owed Joel," Bella said. "He looked positively *pale*. You don't suppose do you, Charlie, there's anything fishy about that note?"

Charlie stared at her, flabbergasted. "Where'd you latch onto that crazy idea?"

"Well, he looked so queer. Wanted to know if I had seen the note; if I were sure it was really Dad's signature. It does seem odd we didn't find any reference to it on the books or among Dad's papers. . . . Where do you suppose all that money could have gone to?"

"No mystery about that," Charlie grumbled, "what with Dallas gettin' into one durn scrape right after another. You don't get that kinda thing hushed up for nothin'."

"Just the same—"

"Now you listen to me, girl! I dunno what kinda malarky that gun-packer's put in your head, but if Joel Kraitch says he loaned Dave twenty thousand you can dang sure bet your boots he done it! He was the best friend your pappy had in this country. *Buen amigos*, they was; all the time visitin' back an' forth till Joe's wife took silly an' run off with that twine salesman. You wouldn't remember about that—you was just button size. Joe was some pumpkins in this part of the cactus before the carryin's-on of that woman, an' the laughin', drove him into his shell. Gave the biggest parties, drunk the most likker—Hell! He may be kinda crotchety now but one thing you can tie to solid: He wouldn't no more set out to skin his old partner's daughter than a hog would have use for a pocket in a bathin' suit."

Which just goes to show even the canniest of ramrods are not without an occasional misjudgment. For at the very time Charlie was making this pronouncement, back at Crazy K headquarters a mousy little man was telling his segundo with a thin-lipped smile, "In a couple more days you can close off that road. We'll be owning every inch of ground between here and the border."

By Bill Downing's watch—and he called this to Alvord's attention with a considerable show of pride—only an hour and ten minutes after leaving the express car the robbers were again picking up their poker hands in the back room of Schweitzer's saloon.

That was pretty fair time for ten miles through the catclaw on barefoot ponies, a complete change of clothing and a two-mile hike through the wind to reach town; but it was no great boost for the telegraph. The operator at Cochise had started heating up the wires before Downing and his accomplices had got the engine rolling. He played hell with that key but he couldn't wake up Willcox. He finally got Bowie out of bed and the man who was taking the night calls for that point promised to get the word to Willcox just as quick as he was able. But the re-coupled train was actually backing into town when the big news came through.

Men poured into the streets like ants from a burning log. From bars and brothels and from the neighboring houses they converged with all the noise of a four-alarm fire. Lord, were they excited! "Stuck up the westbound flyer? *Holy cow!*" Where were those blinkety-blank star packers? Where was that gun toting marshal?

Someone suddenly remembered the card game at Schweitzer's and, shouting and cursing, half the town took out for the place on the run.

Generally Burt Alvord got a lot of fun from his poker but tonight he couldn't keep his mind on the cards. He wasn't worried about Dallas, but knocking Jack Dunlap in the head was an unauthorized complication he hadn't made any allowance for. Trust Stiles to gum things up! And what if the fool had botched it? What if, instead of dead, Three-Fingered Jack had been playing possum!

He could feel the thought churn around through his bowels. Up until now the things he'd done a middling smart man could laugh off, but he had crawled right out on a limb for sure this time. It was no good telling himself he'd practically had to, that after reading Kraitch's note there hadn't been much else he could do; he had used his lawman's knowledge to defraud Wells Fargo of government gold.

He felt acutely uncomfortable, a traitor almost. Yet he knew, if he'd been faced with the same choice again, he would still have laid pipe to get hold of that gold. Kraitch's note had shown him beyond all doubting into what kind of corner the man's scheming had driven her. And when he'd learned the other night from Bella's own lips the appalling size of the debt the man claimed and was demanding, Bert had realized she was whipped.

There was not, in the time Kraitch had left at her disposal, the ghost of a chance Bella Norton could put her hands on twenty thousand dollars. Her crew had been whittled down to where it was nothing but a mockery. The steady drain of Dallas' rustling had reduced the spread's value beyond chance of a profitable sale. When, by an almost unbelievable expenditure of reckless energy, Charlie's skeleton crew had assembled a herd which might have imperiled Kraitch's plans, that maliciously timed and cleverly executed combination raid and stampede had wrecked the girl's final chance.

All the heartbreak and courage, all the hope and dogged struggle she'd put into the fight to save Bar 6 were as nothing—less than nothing—to that two-legged polecat smugly bent on taking over. There'd been a heap too much red blood in Burt's veins to stand idly by and see that son of a bitch ruin her.

When a man's kin are starving he will kill if he has to feed them. Burt had applied the same principle to this thing and sacrificed safety to make Bella safe. The government—or Wells Fargo—could stand the loss a lot better than she could. But he had known when he had hefted those canvas sacks that he had been crossed up again by either Stiles or Downing—perhaps by both of them. He had told them explicitly, before they'd started off, to leave the big "through" safe alone and crack nothing but the "local."

But there was no use raising any sand about it now. Like Stiles' clouting of Dunlap this was just one further hazard, the price of which he would have to pay if, in the additional hue and cry occasioned by it, they were caught.

Looking over the room as he picked up his cards Burt was gratified to see that one man, anyway, had done his job without the addition of uncalled for innovations. The floor around their table was littered with cigarette butts and empty glasses; the place was foul with the smells of whiskey and tobacco smoke.

They were on their third hand when they heard the crowd coming. Burt shoved most of his table cash into the pot, Berts and Downing followed suit and Stiles shoved all of his in, pitching down his cards along with it. When the news-bringers pushed open the door and came barging in things must have looked pretty convincing.

Alvord put on a good show of surprised and outraged indignation when he was able to make out from all their jawing what had happened. Stiles and Downing reached into the pot for their money. Alvord's glance held contempt as he jumped to his feet, grabbing his belts off the chairback and strapping them round him. "To hell with that," he said gruffly. "C'mon—we got work to do!"

He swore in six extras and, ten minutes later, at the head of this posse he was building a dust toward the scene of the holdup. A mile west of Cochise they cut sign with their lanterns and took up the trail. For a ways they could follow the tracks at a gallop but when these turned onto the hard-baked surface of an ancient lake bed, progress was reduced to a snail's pace. But Burt was a tophand at trailing, schooled in this science by old John Slaughter, and he was still dogging sign when it came onto soft ground. Time after time during their tour of the lake bed, long after the others had blasphemously quit, it was Burt who—"like a goddam bloodhound," as one of them put it—always nosed out the trail and led them onward again.

He was indefatigable and patently determined to run those robbers right into a barred cell. But not even his great skill and considerable ingenuity was equal to the chore of following unshod footprints through the maze of tracks surrounding the herd of shod and barefoot ponies hobbled and staked-out along the outer fringes of town. He went over and over and over that ground but was disgustedly forced to call it a night. One of the possemen when he finally dismissed them, fervently assured him nobody could have done any more.

"Any more?" Downing snorted. "Anybody else woulda give up at that lake!"

Willcox next day was bursting at the seams with excited talk and fantastic speculation. Rumor credited the unknown bandits with a haul of $300,000. A Wells Fargo representative was heard to remark that the actual cash value of what they'd gotten away with would not exceed $3,000; but it was noticed by evening that the town was practically "crawling" with Wells Fargo gumshoes. Railroad dicks were all over the place and Sheriff Lewis and his deputies were running around like chickens with their heads off. Burt Alvord, too, was still sniffing after them. He spent the whole day examining the feet of roundabout horses and finally turned up one he swore had been used by the robbers, and the owner agreed with him. He said he had turned the animal out last evening, same as he'd seen others do, on gunnysack hobbles. This morning he hadn't been able to find horse or hobbles. Asked what he did for a living the man presumed he would be classed as a nester.

There were quite a number of bedraggled bits of gunnysack littering the ground roundabout. Alvord called this to his attention. "Any reason for thinkin' you'd know your own if you seen them?"

"I made them from a sack I fetched out here

from Kentucky. I'd know the weave. And there's a mill brand on them."

"An' when'd you first notice the horse had got back?"

"This is the first I've laid eyes on him since yesterday."

"Pretty neat lookin' critter for a plow chaser."

"I haven't heard of any law," the nester mouthed bitterly, "which prohibits a prospective farmer from owning a decent saddler."

The man's apprehension was like a sickness on his face. Alvord smiled at him drily. "She's a hard country, friend." He looked at the horse again. "Was he marked up like this when you turned him out yesterday?"

"Kentuckians don't treat horses like that."

Alvord nodded. "Well, take care of him. An' keep him handy. Might be People's Exhibit A before this thing gits done with."

He was turning away when the man caught his arm. "You don't think I had anything to do with that robbery, do you?"

Alvord looked him over with a whimsical grin. "As a matter of fact, I don't—but I won't be runnin' this show. They're importin' some high-powered talent from outside. Them's the fellers you're goin' to have to watch out for."

That night the robbers assembled at Burt's old adobe, Downing jubilant and bragging, Berts taciturn, Billy Stiles widely grinning as he contemplated various things he intended doing with his share of the loot.

"One thing," Alvord pointed out, "we *don't* want to do is flash any of this money. The town's swarmin' with range dicks. There'll be a lot more an' they'll all be on the lookout for some of this mazuma. They'll have the date an' mintage of every coin in this shipment an' it's apt to go hard with any gent caught passin' one. Alls we've got to do is just sit pat an' keep our mouths shut."

He handed them four hundred and thirty dollars apiece and told them the deal had gone off smooth as silk.

Stiles' jaw hung down like a hoofshaper's apron.

The lanky Texican stared. "I'll take the rest of mine now."

"What rest?" Alvord asked; and Downing's kicked-back chair hit the wall with a clatter.

"A four-way split of eighty thousand smackers comes to twenty thousand bucks an' not a friggin' cent less!"

"Sounds reasonable," Burt nodded. "What's your beef?"

"You know goddam well! I want the rest of my dough!"

"Looks like you might of got your rope kinked a little, Bill. The swamper gets a cut, you know, an' the clothes an' gear never come for free—"

"That don't account for no eighty thousand!" Downing snarled, his look choleric.

"I'm not accountin' for eighty thousand. If you think we made any haul like that you better have a talk with the Wells Fargo agent. I'm basin' this divvy on a total of three thousand."

Berts stowed his share away with a shrug. "Looks like Bill got his trains mixed."

"Mebbe," Stiles rasped, "we been played for suckers!"

Wholly serious, Alvord nodded. "It's had me fightin' my hat to figure where Bill picked up this bum steer in the first place."

He caught the ugly look Downing flashed at Stiles and much that had puzzled him flipped into place. Stiles, he was remembering, had likewise worked for Wells Fargo and had probably been in a position to learn something of the schedules and, the way it shaped up now, he and Downing must have been aiming to jump this train from the very first. But they'd wanted a cat's-paw, hence that auguring with Dallas which had pulled Burt into it.

"Well," he said, holding his face straight, "four hundred an' thirty bucks ain't often got for a couple hours' riding." And he went off with Berts and had a good belly laugh, the first he'd enjoyed since signing on with Bar 6.

THIRTEEN

Quirt and Spur

During the next few days Willcox assumed the frenzied appearance of a boomtown with bed room renting at unheard-of premiums and the hash houses scarcely able to provide enough food to take fair advantage of the upswing in business. Every train, every stage, brought fresh recruits; men came in from the ranches, from the mines and from their homesteads to swell the growing army of reward-hungry searchers. Hardware merchants ran short of cartridges. Livery stables couldn't dig up enough horses and crowbaits changed hands for as high as one hundred dollars. There weren't enough saddles or bridles or blankets. Canteens and water bags fetched whatever price a man cared to name and the outfitters groaned and griped to high heaven every time their bitter eyes fell across their stripped-bare shelves. Dust hung above the town in a choking lemon fog and in the midst of all this lather of activity the Express Company's chief of detectives rolled in on a special coach and took charge without any better luck than all his predecessors.

One of the first men he sent for was the two-gun town marshal, the man who'd been in charge of the original chase. He listened carefully to everything Burt said, rode over the ground with him, talked with Bill Downing, Stiles and Frank Aikens, had a look at the nester's horse and questioned every man who had ridden that night in Burt's posse. He reached the same conclusion all the others had come to. The robbers, after the job, had disappeared into Willcox. He didn't uncover one shred of new evidence. He had no more idea of the bandits' identity than the railroad dicks or any other of the hunters who'd come in from outside. He had no clue whatever as to the whereabouts of the stolen gold.

The descriptions of eye-witnesses were contradictory and worthless. He had talked with the train crew, with the engineer and fireman. He spent three hours with the telegraph operator at Cochise and he got not one solitary inch farther forward than the point at which Burt had left the case the night of the robbery. He wrote a flock of reports and kept everybody sweating but as the minutes and hours and days dragged past it began to look more and more like he'd bumped into the perfect crime.

Burt, however, had latched onto a pair of facts he wasn't sharing with outsiders. Dallas Norton had gone into hiding. And no body had been uncovered in the brush around Cochise Station. Stiles and Downing made discreet inquiries but no one seemed to remember seeing Jack Dunlap around any of his usual haunts in some while. Downing was convinced the frightened pair had quit the country; Stiles said even if they hadn't they'd never dare let out a peep.

But Dunlap, Alvord told himself, if he'd got away under his own power knew Stiles had been concerned. He probably knew Stiles had belted him and, if this were so, he wasn't going to be forgetting it. "He might hook you an' me up with Stiles," Burt told Downing, but the walrus-faced Texican scoffed at such a notion.

"Forget him," he said, as though Jack were just something you could flush down the drain. "He won't air his mug around here no more. If he does it'll be the last time if *I* ketch sight of him!"

Burt was not reassured. Nor was he feeling at all comfortable in his mind about Downing. The guy was too bold, too ready to grab iron if crossed or backed into a corner. He hadn't got over that division yet either and, though he'd done no more growling where Alvord could hear it, he'd developed a disquieting way of watching Burt whenever he figured Burt wasn't aware of it. But the thing which disconcerted Burt most at the moment was the fondness Downing showed for recounting how Alvord had followed those robbers across the baked-hard bottom of that confounded lake. "There was places," he'd say, "where you couldn't find tracks enough to trip up a ant. But that never stopped Burt. He sailed right along till you'd of swore, by God, he was a-readin' their minds!"

Bright and early in the morning of the fifth day following the robbery, barely late enough to make sure of missing the crew, Burt showed up at Bar 6 with a rifle across his knees and a brace of heavy-looking nosebags slung from the horn of his saddle. He wasn't counting on swapping any gas with old Charlie so, after chousing a hasty glance at the horse trap, he pulled up his gelding forty feet from the porch and yelled: "Bella!"

Bella didn't appear and neither did Charlie but Puddin Taylor poked his tousled head from the cook shack. "Save your breath," he growled sourly. "Ain't nobody home but me an' the cactus."

This surprised Burt a little and kind of tightened his mouth corners. When he'd come back here the other night to get the real McCoy on that dough Kraitch claimed was owing him, he had found Bella just about ready for a string of spools. She'd been took so bad with the shakin trembles he'd thought for awhile he wouldn't find out anything; but after she'd had a good cry on his shoulder it had all come out.

About six weeks before, Kraitch had told her he was holding her daddy's note for twenty thousand against the outfit—that was when she had first tried to rope Burt into it and got stuck with Billy Stiles. The cattle kept going. Finally Burt had signed on. Matt Berts had shown up with his rifle and the rustlers had hunted cover; they had been so encouraged Charlie'd started that roundup. Just when they'd thought they might be getting someplace she'd got a note from Kraitch saying he'd have to have his money by the 17th of this month.

Charlie'd told her not to worry; that he'd do the best he was able and with any kind of luck they'd fetch a big enough gather to get the note paid off. It had looked like they were going to when the owlhoots struck again, scattering the cattle and putting Charlie to bed with a hole through his shoulder.

"Buck up," Burt said, "you ain't whipped yet by a jugful. Might take four-five days but I think I can git you out of this. Don't do a thing until you hear from me—savvy? Just set pat an' stick close to the house so's I'll be able to git hold of you."

And that was how he'd left it. Never thinking of course, what with one thing and another, she'd been so tangled in her mind she hadn't half heard him. He'd been some tangled up in his own thinker that night, and her parting kiss hadn't helped matters any.

He squinted at the red-haired cook and chewed

his lip, not much relishing the prospect of touring the range in broad daylight with this pair of bulging grubsacks clanking against his goddam knees.

"What part of the canyon you workin'?" he asked.

Taylor waved a hand southward. "You get a line on them fellers what stuck up that train yet?"

"Took out of my hands. Wells Fargo, the sheriff an' the railroad's roddin' that. Matt Berts out there with 'em?"

"With the crew? Hell, I guess so. He was around last night."

Burt was wondering how it would work to send the cook after Bella, but decided it wouldn't. In this country cooks came next to God in importance and, likely as not, the guy would reach for his meat-axe. He guessed whatever was to be done he would have to do himself. "Didn't reckon ol' Charlie'd be much feelin' like gittin' out an' combin' brush—"

"He ain't with 'em," Taylor said. "Him an' Bella hitched up an' went off in the wagon—Ain't you heard the big news?"

"About 'em ketchin' *Paludo*?"

"No. I meant about Bella—"

"Bella!" Alvord stared at him sharply. "What about her?"

"Why, she's marryin' Kraitch over to Tombstone this mornin'. Ten o'clock sharp. Goin' to throw the two outfits together an'—Christ, man, what's wrong with you?"

Alvord's face looked two shades whiter than caliche. "What time'd she pull outa here?"

"More'n two hou—"

But Burt was already gone, quirting and spurring like hell wouldn't have him.

FOURTEEN

A Busted Flush

When Alvord astride a foam-flecked gelding came tearing into Tombstone at three minutes of ten, batting the yellow dust hat high as he went larruping past Fly's Photo Shop on the final lap of his desperate drive to reach the steepled church just beyond Safford's crossing, the clanking nosebags were no longer slung from his saddle. Where they had gone is anybody's guess but he certainly did not have them with him.

He was onto the ground before the horse could stop, skidding on creaking bootheels. The doors slammed open under the crash of his shoulder. Stained glass threw multicolored light across the pew backs but Burt's bitter eyes took a full five thumping heartbeats to knock it into his skull that, except for himself, the silent church was empty.

He had never before realized a place could feel so cold, or that cold could be the color of fear.

He backed through the doors like a man in his sleep and stood uncertainly on the steps, still staring but not seeing, while the sun's bright shafts drove some warmth into his shoulders. He scrubbed a hand across his face as though

159

to brush away a cobweb and was wheeling toward his horse when a boy's shrill voice cried derisively, "You got the wrong place, mister. Christ only works in there on Sundays."

Alvord peered at him stupidly. He had the uncomfortable impression he might be seeing himself in that barefooted urchin. "Huntin' the sky pilot," he muttered. "Don't suppose you'd know—"

"Where he is? Betcha boots I do! He's got a knot-splicin' on over to the rectory. You figgerin' to break it up?"

"Show me where," Alvord said.

The kid drew him off to one side and pointed. "Right there—that house behind them umbrella trees—see it? They're prob'ly about through by—"

Alvord flipped him a coin and broke into a run. The urchin's grubby hand snatched the glint in midflight and his eyes opened wide when he saw the coin's color. "Jeez!" he breathed reverently, and started running himself.

The rector said: "Do you, Bella Madeline Norton, take this man—" and stopped with mouth open as booted feet struck the porch and a savage hand all but jerked the screen door off its hinges. Bella gasped and Kraitch swore; and the old man very nearly dropped his book. Limned against the brightness of that outside glare Alvord's

160

burly shape must, in the ecclesiastic's startled mind, have epitomized all the blasphemy and violence of the town's hectic past. He swallowed with understandable distaste and, abruptly recalling his orders, said: "If you can't employ circumspection at least show a little respect for my cloth. If you will take off that hat and stand quietly now, I will get on with the Lord's—"

"You got a heap more gall than savvy," Alvord panted, "if you're figurin' to shunt this deal off on God."

Roughly thrusting a pair of frightened witnesses aside, and giving no concern whatever to the scowling face of Charlie, he bent a bleak look on the whey-cheeked rancher.

"I ain't the kind, generally speaking, to go rammin' my spoon in another gent's soup, but if you think Bella Norton's cravin' to git herself hitched to any guy old enough to be her gran'father, you better take another squint. I can see it's high time you was told a few things, Reverend, so I'll give it to you straight. This skunk," he said, jerking a contemptuous thumb at Kraitch, "is low-down enough to tote a bucket of sheep-dip. He could eat off the same plate with a snake an' never notice—"

"If you think," Kraitch spluttered, "I have to stand around and listen—"

"You'll listen, all right, or you'll be headin' for a dentist to git your bridle teeth fixed. This whelp," Burt told the preacher, "has been smugglin' dope for years. It has gravelled him plenty to have to antigoddle round to git the stuff past Bar 6 but so long as Bella's dad was alive he hadn't much choice. Old Norton's kids however was somethin' else again an', soon as the place got out of the courts, he made the girl an offer. She turned him down so he got to work on her brother; fed him this hemp an' started the kid to rustlin' her stock. When that didn't show rough enough he set one of his gunslicks to killin' off the crew; he'd of had her then but I took chips an' that kinda crimped the cuttin' edge of his shovel.

"Don't be throwed by that sneer. You're starin' at a guy which is twice as slick as slobbers. When his bunch of drygulchers took to huntin' their holes, this fine upstandin' rancher reshuffles his rigged deck an' deals himself the joker—a note of hand for twenty grand which he claims packs ol' Dave's crow tracks.

"Now he's got her pinned down to where she can't hardly wiggle. He has Charlie here fooled same's he had Bella's daddy an' is bankin' high she'll be too proud to let me know what he's up to. Then he says he's caught short an' is going to have to ask her to pick up that note, knowin' she can't square it short of givin' him the ranch.

"Charlie's still got a little steam left. He takes up his crew—the four hands them rustlers ain't planted—an' starts to roundin' up the pastures. That's a plumb rugged country where they have to work these cattle an' this dirty flop-eared hound"—eyeing Kraitch—"sets back to lick his greasy chops. With time, the country an' their own short-handedness all workin' for him it's a cinch he's got them boxed, an' knows it.

"Them boys put in two weeks of tophand labor but this bugger had 'em whipsawed. When they'd built up a gather which might of pulled Bar 6 from under, Kraitch rings in his hired guns an' stampedes the herd from hell to breakfast. That's the story in a nutshell. He's got the spread if he can git away with it an', to make sure he does, he's got this trump you was all set to hand him. It's as slick a swindle as you're like to meet up with. To keep from gettin' throwed out the girl's got to marry this two-legged polecat. An' that's why she's here."

"You ought to pass around the salt," Kraitch sneered, "when you tell that one," but the preacher's complacency appeared considerably shaken. Doubt leached through from the backs of his eyes and there was something askance in his regard of the rancher that darkened Kraitch's cheeks with an upswing of fury.

"You swallerin' that pack of lies?" he demanded.

The rector, though plainly unaccustomed to scenes of this nature, was a staunch man at heart;

163

and he said now to Alvord, "Do you have proof of these things?"

"I can show you the letter he wrote askin' for payment. Charlie here, and the crew, can tell you all you want to know about the rustlin', those killin's and the stampedin' of that herd. He overplayed his hand when he run off them cattle—give himself away like a shirtful of fleas. The boys dropped three of the bunch he had with him that night an' one of them Berts recognized—"

"You think," Kraitch said with an ugly laugh, "anyone's going to take that feller's word—"

"They'll take it," Alvord grinned, "when I produce the pair of rannies I latched onto this mornin' goin' into your place with a load of raw—"

Kraitch moved fast but not fast enough. His gun was just coming out of leather when flame burst whitely from Alvord's hand. The rancher, staggering backward, struck the wall but it wouldn't hold him. He was past all talk forever when he settled against the floor.

FIFTEEN

Marked Man

When Alvord set out upon the long ride to Willcox, after seeing Bella Norton home, he had plenty of food for reflection and not all of it by any means pleasant. One thing he didn't regret was Kraitch's passing though Charlie, even by the time they'd got halfway to Bar 6, appeared to find it tough sledding to believe an old friend could be as bad as Burt painted him.

"He never was your friend, nor Bella's; an' if that note was on the level what'd he drag that gun for? He knew damn well I was onto him—that's why!"

"And do you truly think," Bella asked, mighty wistful, "it was Kraitch all the time behind that rustling instead of Dallas?"

" 'Course it was Kraitch; I don't think your brother's even around this stretch of cactus. That guy's been tryin' to git hold of your spread for years; tried to buy it off your daddy an' one time almost had him talked into it. When Dave went, he tried to get you to sell. When he didn't git crackin' on that line either he recollected them windy threats Dallas made and, just that quick, you find yourself buckin' rustlers. There ain't

165

a doubt in my mind it was Kraitch had your waddies dropped."

"Be a hard thing to prove," old Charlie said skeptically and, a little later, "I jest can't get it outa my craw there's a heap more to this'n I was able to ketch onto."

"You're worse than a treeful of owls," Burt had snorted. "You got that note off your neck, you're done losin' cattle; all your troubles is ironed out. What you squawkin' about?"

"I'd like to be able to live with my conscience—"

"Why, you ungrateful ol' reprobate! How much conscience do you reckon Kraitch had?"

"I don't have to worry about his," the old man answered. He sat hunched forward on the wagon seat, elbows on knees, morosely staring over the rumps of the plodding horses. Bella, too, had grown silent, but hers was more a tired kind of quiet as though she'd put all thought aside and was taking what content she could from knowing the worst was over.

But Charlie was like a dog with a bone. "It's too pat," he grumbled. "I don't expect to see a package wrapped up that neat. I keep wonderin' what it'll look like if it gets bumped around a little."

Alvord scowled, saying nothing, but the old man wouldn't leave it alone. "You said Joe was back of that rustlin'. You called him a smuggler;

claimed he was runnin' dope an' you had just caught two of his boys—"

"What about it?"

"I don't see how you could of done that. You had to come out from Willcox. You see an' grab a couple of guys goin' into Joe's place with what you've told us was contraband. Then you drop south to our place, discover we ain't home, find out where we've gone to and what we've gone to do there. You climb outa the canyon, make the dash north an' east—which I've never done yet in under two solid hours—and pull into Tombstone, locate where we're at and manage to halt the proceedings all by a few minutes after ten o'clock. What was you ridin'—a couple of twisters?"

"I left home pretty early."

"You musta left in the middle of the night to make that time!"

"Any objection?"

"Don't bristle at me, you conscienceless gunhawk!" Charlie's eyes were black agate. "You was lyin' through your teeth when you told him you caught—"

"Sure I was, but it worked. You seen him go for his gun—"

"I'd of gone for mine too if I'd figured you was framin'—"

"Charlie!" Bella cried. "I won't have you talking that way! If it hadn't been for Burt—"

"Didn't you hear him just admit he talked Kraitch into—"

"I don't care!"

Charlie sucked in his breath. "I thank God your ol' pappy—"

"I'm not a child!" Bella flared. "You heard what Burt said. Joel made up that note, just as I thought he did. He brought in those rustlers. He stampeded my cattle—"

"Two wrongs don't make no right in my book. No matter what Kraitch done—"

Alvord, leaning from the saddle, tapped the old man's shoulder. "Who you workin' for—Kraitch or Miz Bella?"

"Get your hand offa me!" Charlie twisted around, showing Alvord his back and saying grimly to Bella, "Pay this guy off an' get rid of him."

"Why?"

"Because he ain't our kind of people!"

Of all the talk exchanged during that ride it was this remark which cut Burt deepest, calling up bitter memories from out of the past when as a kid it had so frequently been a door closed against him, shutting him out of the privileges commonly accorded more fortunate friends until, in rebellion, he had found his own level among the tarpaper shacks and pool halls.

"That's a fine thing to say"—Bella's voice was indignant—"after all Burt has done for us!"

"He'll git paid for what he's done—"

"Some things, Charlie, can't be bought with cash."

"He can!" The old man glared at Burt blackly. "I don't want him around. I'd as soon have a tiger holed up in the bunkhouse. We got no place at Bar 6 for—"

"Then we'll make a place," Bella said with her chin up.

The old man jumped from his seat like she'd stabbed him. "Hell's fire, girl! Ain't you seen the truth yet? Ain't you ketched the wild bunch smell on him? He rowelled Joe into drawing so's he could gun him down like you would a mad dog!"

Bella's eyes were burnt holes staring out of white cheeks. "I can't believe that," she whispered. "Joel brought his death on himself by—"

"I ain't goin' to argy the matter," Charlie snapped. "Bar 6 ain't big enough for both of us. It's your spread an' your choice but if you keep him on you won't need me."

Alvord watched the shock of that bite into her and thought for a little she would break down and bawl. Her face got all funny. She threw out a hand blindly and then, when he grasped what her choice was going to be, Burt said tightly: "No need for that, Charlie. I'm swingin' out of this deal right here."

169

• • •

Burt came into Willcox, on the day following Kraitch's death, a little before noon to find the town so crammed with detectives there was hardly enough room to draw a full-sized breath. Nor was he kept long in doubt as to what manner of thing had fetched them. Downing, tanked up, had made a tour of the community's honkytonks and dead-falls blatantly ringing gold eagles on the bars and, as though that were not bad enough, a pair of these outside investigators had been found dead as doornails in one of the town's back alleys.

Sheriff Lewis had come over from Tombstone and the brass-collar dog of the Wells Fargo crowd had come back from Cochise and they were grilling Downing now in Schweitzer's back room. No one asked Burt Alvord to sit in on it. So he rode the streets in his capacity as marshal, apparently oblivious of the many covert glances which his presence was attracting.

He carried it off well. No one could have guessed how near he was to bolting or how bleakly tight his muscles were. He knew suspicion would have already spread to Berts and Stiles as well as to himself and that a single jumpy move right now would put the fat in the fire for sure. They would all be watched like hawks for a while and this knowledge brought home to him as nothing else could have how far

170

he had strayed from the straight and narrow since that day he had met Bella Norton in Tombstone's Cosmopolitan Hotel.

He was not blaming anyone. He understood now something of what Charlie'd meant when he'd said last night, "He ain't our kind of people." He guessed he wasn't at that though it was hard to put your finger on just where the difference started. Maybe he'd always been different, he thought, scowling. Then he brushed that away. He had more important things to think about.

At half past three he woke up Aikens who'd be packing the tin until eleven that night. Frank was full of the story of Downing's parade with the gold pieces. "You reckon he got 'em off that train like they're hinting?"

"Dunno," Burt said. "It don't look like he'd be fool enough to go flashin' them if he did."

But you never knew what a guy would do with a load on. It had taken Bella's departure for Tombstone yesterday morning to remind him how near he'd come to pulling a bigger boner than Downing. Bella's ramrod would have been suspicious pronto if he had thumped those nosebags full of coins on their verandah. With all Burt's careful figuring he had never considered that angle. He had saved all his worry for the gold's effect on the Crazy K owner, finally concluding that Kraitch with his hemp trade had been on much too thin ice to risk involving himself with the law about anything.

As he rode the two miles to his house on the flats he kept pondering his past, trying to dredge up the answer to the difference Charlie'd found in him. It was sorry work and the yield insignificant to a man who, for as long as he could remember, had been most bent on "belonging." It was the way he'd tripped Kraitch that had got under Charlie's hide, but Burt couldn't see anything in that to work a sweat up. Joe Kraitch had been the kind of sidewinder that any right-thinking feller had ought to been glad to put a heel on; a dealer in dope, a guy who'd waxed fat off a drug known to turn people loco. Of course Burt had aimed to wind up Kraitch's string—what of it? The law couldn't get at Joe and Burt had done nothing more than prod him into action. Kraitch hadn't had to drag that gun; he could have fled and still been alive now. It had been his own choice which had got the bastard planted. And a damned good choice all around!

Burt could see, though, a few of the milestones his own spurred boots had gone dashing past. From the lark of running off Papago ponies to the more arduous game of chousing Mexican cattle into gringo ovens had been a simple and quite natural progression. Plenty of gents in these localities had made the same move and been thought none the worse of. It wasn't perhaps

172

exactly right but who the hell bothered to be exact anyway?

There was, unfortunately, this thing of progression.

An astonishing discovery. In his travels through the tenderloin regions of these districts he had noticed most drinkers generally tended to start with an occasional small one but a lot of these folks, inside a couple years, would be putting the stuff away about as fast as the apron could pour it. Progression again. A kind of pattern in behavior which a lot of numps called "habit."

Burt was suddenly discovering it entered into just about every last thing a man could set his hand to. Take Bill Hickok now, or Bonney—nice a pair as you'd hope to meet until they'd took to killing. Seemed like one thing always led to another and he guessed that was how it had been with him. Running off Indian ponies hadn't been anything to get excited about. Lifting Mexican longhorns hadn't seemed much different—nor had he lost any sleep while entertaining the prospect of stopping that train. Seemed the natural thing to do when you considered it.

Badness, evidently, was subject to progression also.

Burt took a good long look right then toward where he was headed. "Jesus Christ!" he said, and whistled. Sweat cracked through the backs of his hands and broke out where his knees gripped the barrel of his horse.

Like the nails going down the sides of a coffin he caught a glimpse of past acts in their true proportion from those jugheaded broncs straight down to Kraitch's killing; he never had been so shocked in his life. It kind of looked like he'd better start to pulling leather pronto if he didn't aim to end up as a cottonwood blossom.

He'd just one bright spot to tie to: The remembrance that Bella Norton had been going to let Charlie go.

SIXTEEN

Tombstone

As other men had before him, Alvord found that closing a stable after the horse had gotten away did not butter many parsnips. About all he was able to do for the moment was sit tight and keep his mouth shut.

It was obvious enough Wells Fargo suspected which were the wolves in sheep's clothing. But suspicion and proof, as Burt had learned chasing Kraitch, can be sometimes right difficult to join up with evidence. Four months had dragged past and they still hadn't got enough to jail even Downing.

Time and again they had dug up the floor of Burt's lonesome adobe, they'd worked over the yard and jerked every fencepost for a full mile around, but all they had got to show for this labor was a one-dollar watch packed into a tomato can and tied with pink ribbon which one of the detectives had turned up in Burt's chicken run.

Everyone was howling for action and the Wells Fargo dicks were still getting nowhere along with the snoopers sent in by the railroad when Governor Murphy, who'd got fed up with crooks, sent for Burt Mossman and told him to organize a company of Rangers. Mossman, who had managed the Hashknife and cleaned all the rustlers away from the Blue, said he was just about beginning to get his own affairs in order and how about asking someone else. All the big guns in the Territory got after him and Col. Randolph said he ought to think of Arizona and the Southern Pacific; and in the end he gave in. So now it looked like, in addition to all the scalp-hunting pilgrims already on the job, Alvord and his train-robbing friends would mighty soon be having to contend with Territorial Rangers.

Downing, these days, after all the badgering he'd had from Wells Fargo, had turned tight-lipped and ugly. But the Express Company wasn't quitting and finally they got hold of a fellow who had once ridden shotgun guard with Stiles. After explaining the situation they said: "We don't care how you do it, but you work on this ranny and see if you can't get him to open up a little. Downing's spent gold that came off of that train and the closest friends he's got in this town are Stiles, Matt Berts and Alvord. It's a cinch all four of them were in on it. You get the goods on that bunch and we'll see you're taken care of."

"But why me?" this fellow asked.

"Because," they said, "we've done everything but stand on our heads and we haven't got one blasted bit of proof yet. We've turned Bill

Downing inside out and got nowhere. Berts won't say a word and Alvord just laughs at us."

"You want a conviction, eh?"

"Conviction be damned! We want to get back that money! If we're ever to get our hands on it we'll have to do it through Stiles—"

"More your line than mine, ain't it?"

"Never mind that. Pumping Stiles is the last chance we've got and we can't afford to bungle it. I've kept all the boys away from him; but an old friend like you, a feller that's worked with Billy and been around him long enough to understand what he will go for and won't, had ought to be able to get the job done. You can have a free hand, work it anyway you want; promise him anything. If we can get enough to slap the rest of that bunch in jail, one of them may try to bargain his way out and give us a chance to recover that gold."

Accordingly, one crisp winter day on which a man couldn't speak without his breath getting ahead of him, a flashy looking gent climbed down off the train, handsomely tipped a grinning porter and reclaimed his baggage. Toting it through the station he cut grandly through the ruts of the street on his spurless handstitched Hyers and went into the Willcox Hotel where he described himself as a clothing salesman and went into his act with a wealth of fine gestures.

He didn't go hunting the chunky, dark-complected Stiles but left it to the latter to discover his presence, which Billy did the following morning. They shook hands warmly and swapped bull for awhile, then the Wells Fargo man took Stiles into a bar and poured a few slugs of high-priced mouth-rinser down him. Billy thawed considerable and they discussed old times when they'd both rode guard for the Express Company. "How come you to be in this sissified business?" Billy finally asked, and his old friend slapped his thigh with a laugh.

"Man, this has got packing a gun beat all hollow! No scrimping and no worrying about getting potted. And the dough rolls in just like out of a mixer. I'll sell every nob in this town one of these— Here, lemme show you," and he opened his case and fetched out his samples.

"Feel this! Ever see anything like it? The Prince of Wales himself ain't got a thing that can touch it—wear like iron, the color won't fade and you can take it through a cloudburst and never lose an inch! Gives a man class and distinction. Designed by experts. And the girls—God bless 'em—they just can't keep away from it—Gil Crestner says he has to fight 'em off with a club!

"Sold six of them to that belted earl at the Matador last week. Sold the head of your Vigilance Committee one yesterday. Del Lewis ordered one and that feller that runs the bank here—"

"How much do they set a feller back?" Stiles asked.

"You won't ever miss it, chum. And with a build like you got you can knock 'em for a loop! Hell—you know what my boss calls this line? *Calico Catchers!*" He jabbed Stiles' ribs with a gusty elbow. "You know what a natty dresser Colonel Bill Greene is? He won't wear nothing else—been orderin' them for years. Nope, you just can't go wrong with a suit made by Chalpser—thirty-two different cuts and weaves to pick from."

He pawed through his samples, finally found the one he was hunting and held it up against Billy's shoulder. "How you like that for shade?"

Stiles licked his lips. "I kinda thought that light blue—"

"This herringbone? You'd look better with a softer weave. I've got that same shade—here! There—how do you like that? Jay Gould never wore a better piece of goods. You want two pairs of trousers?" he asked, getting out his tape and measuring Billy on the spot.

"What the hell," Stiles asked, "would I do with two pair? Wear one of 'em to bed?"

"If you happened to get one pair ripped or wanted to get them pressed—"

"You must think I'm Ed Tovrea. One pair's aplenty! When you got to have the cash?"

"Well, there's no particular hurry. I expect I'll

be around here all the rest of the week more than likely."

"Sixty bucks you said, didn't you? I'll fetch it round to your room tomorrow night. Say about nine—that all right?"

"Fine as silk. I'll lay in some good Scotch and we'll have a real bull session."

But when Stiles showed up the next night, as promised, and dropped six ten-dollar gold pieces in the supposed salesman's hand, the Wells Fargo man considered him with a rather dubious look and said, "By gollies, Bill, I don't know whether I ought to take this or not. According to some talk I overheard this evening you probably won't be having much use for that suit," and he pushed back the coins with a doleful sigh.

Stiles' mouth dropped open. "What the hell is this?"

"Well, you maybe haven't noticed it but this here burg is plumb crawling with dicks and it looks like they've got you figured for a train robber. Some feller called Downing is going to spill his guts and—"

Stiles swore a blue streak. He really made a job of it, describing Downing's ancestry in meticulous and profane detail. "He'll have to move damn spry if he aims to beat me!" he snarled and, dashing from the room, he went down the stairs like a herd of wild horses, the Wells Fargo yarn-spinner puffing to keep up.

They rushed straight to the office of the local magistrate who, taking off his glasses, peered at Stiles suspiciously. But Billy had his dander up and was not minded to stop at half measures now.

"Judge," he gasped, panting. "I wanta make a confession—"

"You're five minutes too late."

"What!" Stiles shouted, almost beside himself. "You mean to say that goddam Downing's already shot his—"

"My good man, control yourself. You think I work at this job all night? Come around in the morning if you've got anything to say to me."

He squirmed into his coat and was picking up his hat when Stiles caught his arm. "By grab," he snarled, "you better listen to me an' listen right now if you want to get back the money that was took off that flyer!"

The judge hesitated, frowning. "You mean you think you know—"

"Think hell! I was in on it!"

The old man reluctantly put down his hat, told his clerk to fetch a notebook and pencil and, when all was ready, Stiles shot his bolt, withholding nothing save the parts played by Dunlap and Dallas. But while they were waiting around for the clerk to ready a copy for Billy's signature, Burt Alvord flung open the door and rushed in.

"Bill, you damn fool—what do you think you're up to?"

Stiles backed off, glowering; and the side door flipped open showing a pair of Wells Fargo dicks with sawed-off Greeners pointed square at Burt's middle. "You're under arrest, Alvord!" rasped the supposed clothing salesman—"and anything you care to say will be used in evidence against you!"

"Under arrest for what?"

"Your connection with the robbery of the westbound flyer on the night of September 11—"

"I don't know what kind of guff Stiles has fed you," Alvord snorted, "but I can tell you right now you'll play hell hookin' me up with—"

"That injured look ain't going to buy you a thing," the pseudo suit drummer grinned. "You're a cooked goose, bucko. Billy Stiles has confessed—"

"An' you fell for it?" Burt shook his head like he felt sorry for them. "Don't you savvy that poor lunkhead would do anything for attention? He had no more chance to stick up that train—"

"You might's well save it for the jury. You ain't selling me a thing."

A clatter of boots came pounding up the stairs and the top screw of the Wells Fargo dicks burst in with six or eight more of his men on his heels. "Nice work, boy," he cried enthusiastically; "I was sure you could do it. Take the guns off him, Joe. Bob, you and Clarence hold this fellow under wraps. I want the rest of you boys to get out and round up Berts and Downing. Soon's we've got them in the bag I'll send the whole outfit over to Tombstone under escort—"

But he was wrong about that. His detectives picked up Downing without any trouble but Berts had left town and could not be located; so the only ones who went to Tombstone next morning with the heavily armed escort were Bill Downing and Alvord who were carefully confined in separate steel-barred cells.

When booked, Willcox's marshal declared the whole thing was a frameup, a deplorable miscarriage of justice which the authorities wouldn't live down in a coon's age. He insisted he had not robbed any train and Downing refused to say anything.

All manner of stories were riding the winds and it was apparent that Alvord was not without friends. Quite a number of these, including several solid citizens, considered it hysterical to accuse old Burt of having had any hand in what had happened to the flyer. That feller Downing perhaps and maybe even Matt Berts; but where was the sense trying to pin it on Alvord just because he'd been friendly with a couple of hard characters? He was on talking terms with most of the country's undesirables, and had been for years; had gone out of his way to achieve this condition as an adjunct to packing the tin for John Slaughter. Only a fool would ever hold that against him.

Some people felt the whole thing was a mare's nest, an enormous red herring cooked up by Billy Stiles. Many favored the notion this was another of Alvord's pranks, some gigantic hoax he was furthering to get a laugh on Wells Fargo.

A number of the Express Company officials were privately inclined to take this same view, particularly since Stiles—after discovering how he'd been played for a sucker—had refused to sign his confession.

Matt Berts had finally come in and surrendered, but all they could get out of him was that Stiles had taken advantage of his strained public relations to implicate him in a crime he'd had nothing whatever to do with.

Though Stiles' confession without his signature was worthless as legal evidence, the authorities continued to hold the suspected men in custody while the Wells Fargo sleuths, the railroad dicks, the sheriff's deputies and all the rest of the scalp and glory hunters indefatigably combed the terrain again. Time after time the prisoners were questioned—frequently for two and three hours at a crack—but without advancing even the ghost of a solution. Berts and Downing kept their lips firmly buttoned and neither threats nor bribery got a single admission out of them. Alvord treated the whole thing as a kind of a lark, laughing and joking with all who came near him. He arranged for his horses to be well taken care of, insisting they be given their regular ration of grain. "Them broncs ain't robbed no train, by grannies, an' it ain't right they should get shortchanged on their groceries. I want 'em fetched past the window every day so's I can see they're bein' treated right."

He ate heartily himself on money owing from his marshal's job and spent the bulk of his time in whittling. He carved a whole herd of mighty lifelike horses and one day fashioned a ludicrous likeness of the boss Wells Fargo dick turning over stones—"Huntin'," he told callers, "for that missin' three thousand."

If he was worried he didn't show it. And he managed very cleverly to one day cue Berts and Downing while the three were being exercised, remarking casually, "Gettin' throwed in clink never hurt nobody that didn't have it comin' to him. God takes care of His own—that's gospel. An' when a man's really innercent he's got no cause for goin' off his head if he'll only remember that right always triumphs. Take us, for instance. That feller Stiles has made things look mighty black but if these dicks poke around long enough they'll learn the truth, an' the truth'll git us outa here. Actually them fellers has got nothin' at all against us. They can't railroad a feller just for havin' a few coins that come out of that express car—they got to prove first of all that he personally took 'em outa there. That's goin' to take some doin'. All three of us was right there in Schweitzer's playin' cards when that dough was lifted; an' they can't get around that if they try from now till doomsday."

He might not have been quite so confident had he known that one of Mossman's Rangers—a persevering gent named Grover—had broken down that alibi. He'd done this within a couple of days after Stiles' confession but was keeping it to himself because he wasn't able to prove it and Stiles' confession, without his signature, wasn't worth the paper used to record it. Grover had gotten to work on the swamper who had set up the props while the boys were away. But the terrified negro, after admitting his part in it, had taken a powder and dug for the tules.

The law was convinced they had jailed the right parties but was no nearer proving it than they had been when they'd grabbed them. And this still was the situation when, on the night of February 17th, a second train was stopped—this one at Fairbank.

SEVENTEEN

The Reckless People

Berts and Downing were jubilant when they heard about this but Alvord, sensing what must have occurred, was not too inclined to consider it a blessing, particularly after learning one of the robbers had been wounded. If, as he supposed, Dallas and Dunlap were back of this the eventual result might prove anything but helpful to the men who had hijacked the pair's first attempt.

Jeff Milton, who had been a Texas ranger, was lounging in the open doorway of the express car when the train was stopped. He hadn't realized what was happening until a man stepped up out of the darkness and gruffly commanded him to "Climb down outa that car!"

Instead of obeying, he tried to get the doors shut and took a bullet in the arm. Before the bandit could fire again Jeff grabbed up his shotgun and filled the fellow full of buckshot. Then he threw away the keys and all the outlaws got for their trouble was a paltry thirty-five dollars.

A couple of days later Burt's uncomfortable premonition was shown to have had considerable foundation when it was learned in Tombstone that on the previous afternoon the man shot by Milton had been discovered and identified.

"Discovered where?" Alvord asked.

"Along the trail those highbinders took makin' their getaway."

"Who was the guy?"

"Small-timer named Dunlap. You ever hear of him?"

Burt scrubbed a hand across his jaw and said reluctantly, "As a matter of fact, if it's the gent I'm thinkin' of, I had a run-in with him a couple or three years ago when I was workin' undercover for the Border Control. I come within a ace of hangin' ten years on him. This galoot was known as 'Three-Fingered Jack.' "

"Same man, I expect. One of his dewclaws didn't have all its grubhooks on it."

"Small world," Alvord grunted. "You say they found him dead—"

"I expect his crowd figured he was a goner and cut loose of him but he wasn't actually dead when we got to him."

"I'm sure glad of that," Burt said fervently. "He'll have told you enough that you can drop them charges you been—"

"He ain't come to, yet, an' it don't look like he's going to. Mystery to me the guy is able to keep on breathin' with all that buckshot Milton pumped into him; couldn't have been more'n two horse-lengths away by the look of him. Doc claims he's hangin' on by sheer determination—thinks he's got something on his mind."

"Grudge, more than likely. Prob'ly riled," Alvord said, "the way his pals rode off an' left him. You never got a thing, eh?"

"I guess you'll hear about what we got when the sheriff comes round to talk to you. He's closeted with some of those Wells Fargo gents but he'll likely be along as soon as he gets rid of them—and," the Southern Pacific man said significantly, "if you've got anything to tell us you had better have it ready."

The day dragged past without the sheriff coming near him.

Burt suspected this whole deal was a carefully prepared play to work on his nerves so that when Del Lewis should finally get to him he would be softened up enough to be ready to talk turkey. Burt had watched John Slaughter employ this trick many times and it almost always worked.

It wasn't going to work with him, Burt assured himself; but that didn't keep him from sweating. Everything that dick had told him could have been pure bull. He didn't believe it was but he had no way of guessing how much of the story had been truth and how much hokum. The guy had passed out Dunlap's name but even that could have been a red herring.

Burt didn't sleep so well that night. He got up

feeling like he'd been dragged through a knothole and had to force himself to eat when the guard fetched round his breakfast. It was all he could do to keep from pacing his cell.

At nine o'clock the jailor came in and told him to prepare for company, and that in itself was a source of irritation because most of the time they simply fetched the company in without a by-your-leave or anything else. He wished he could swap a few words with Berts and Downing but there never had been any chance to do so privately; no other prisoners were being held in this block and there were too many vacant cells between them to hold conversation without some guard overhearing it.

Expecting to see Del Lewis he was set back on his heels when he looked up and found Bella Norton in the corridor. For several moments they stood eyeing each other without speaking and then, as though there were no one in the place but themselves, Bella came forward and put her face against the bars. "Burt! Oh, my—"

"Careful," Burt said without moving his lips, "that guard's got his ears cocked—"

"But it's ridiculous to hold you any longer; I've told them so. There couldn't be two gangs of train robbers working in this country and how could—I thought even Del Lewis would be smart enough to know you couldn't very well—"

"There's been another train stopped?"

"Just the other night at Fairbank—Didn't you know?"

"Tell me."

"There were several men mixed up in it just as there were that first time. When they tried to get into the express car one of them was shot. This fellow, a man named Dunlap, was found the next day, badly wounded and delirious—"

"What did he say?"

"It isn't known. They're keeping him closely guarded—"

"He's still alive then?"

"I think so. I want you to know you've got friends outside and they're working for you—"

"The way you feel is all that matters to me. If I get clear of this, Bella—"

"Oh, my dear, you will! I'm sure you will—and soon now! Some of your friends have got up a petition and—"

"Will you wait for me, Bella?"

She looked into his anxious eyes and said, "Of course. All my life if—"

"Time's up, Miss," the guard said, touching her shoulder. "You'll have to go now."

She caught Burt's hands through the bars and gripped them tightly.

Del Lewis dropped around that afternoon with a lean hard-twisted man in clothes that looked as if they'd seen a deal of riding. Del introduced the

191

man as 'Grover' but did not say he was a Ranger. Grover didn't mention it, either. He told Burt frankly what he'd learned from the swamper. "It ties in," he said, "with what Stiles has told us."

Burt went on with his whittling, not bothering to look up.

The Ranger cleared his throat. "I wouldn't count too heavy on that Fairbank job clearin' you. Your name was included in what we got from Dunlap."

Burt kept right on carving just as though he hadn't spoken.

"You ain't kiddin' nobody!" Del Lewis said hotly. "This is the last chance I'm givin' you. If you want to get out of there talk an' talk quick!"

Burt put up his jackknife. "Mr. Lewis," he said quietly, "my record speaks for itself. If this Dunlap feller had said anything against me you wouldn't be out here tryin' to scare me with it. I haven't stopped any trains. I haven't robbed any trains. And I might remind you that what a man says when he is out of his head is not legal evidence. You haven't one damn piece of legal evidence against me."

The sheriff's face got red and he swelled up like a carbuncle and while he was trying to find enough spit to talk with, Alvord declared, "I'm going to be frank with you, Lewis. I've got you an' this county between a rock and the hard place.

If I should start a action for unwarranted arrest and forcible detention you might find it pretty tough sleddin' to scrape up enough to pay your share of the damages."

Late that night, and with all the stealth possible, another man was fetched in and given a cell in the special all-steel block shared by Alvord, Berts and Downing. This was an exceptionally tall powerfully-built kind of man with great hands and long arms and a bristling mustache that was black and stiff as the tail hair of a horse. Six deputies flanked his entrance and three more came in after him, all armed to the teeth although his wrists were heavily manacled and stout rope hobbles were fastened about his boot-covered ankles. In the light of the corridor lantern his eyes gleamed wild as a stallion bronc's and a shiver ran down Burt Alvord's back as, even without his tangle of whiskers, he recognized this was Augustin Chacon, the fiercest *bandido* ever to come out of Mexico.

Two afternoons later the sheriff visited Burt again. He came alone this time and one glance at his face was enough to convince Burt he had not come to release him. There was a jubilant glint of triumph behind the lawman's bleak stare and a considerable amount of personal satisfaction. "Thought you might like to know your pal

Dunlap has kicked off—but not before we got his signed statement."

"All right. Get it off your chest," Alvord said. "No matter how many lies that sorry son's told, you've still got to find thirteen men who'll believe them."

"Don't pin no hope on that," Lewis grinned. "A deathbed confession packs a lot of weight in this country."

"The guy was out of his head," Burt scoffed.

"Be a damned cold day when you sell that to anyone! He named the whole gang and your name, Alvord, is second on the list! We're going to hold you and Downing over for the Grand Jury—"

"More waste of the taxpayers' money. Just what does this two-bit crook claim I done?"

"He says you planned both jobs and took an active part in the first one—"

"I can see you readin' that in court," Burt chuckled.

"I'll read it—"

"But you won't make it stick."

"It'll stick all right," the sheriff rasped angrily, "when Grover tells what he got from that swamper and we tie it all in with Stiles' signed statement!"

"You're a bigger ass than I took you for. Why, I'll laugh you out of court with that stuff. All you've got, Del, is a pile of damn words—the words of a pair of self-confessed train robbers. You haul me into court with that crap an' I'll make you look the biggest fool in Arizona."

"We'll see about that!" Lewis snapped and, with a final bleak stare, tramped off up the corridor.

Burt was a heap less confident than he'd been making out; but so were the interests leagued against him. At the Wells Fargo office in Willcox a large man in a soft black hat was bitterly inspecting the sullen face of Billy Stiles. This was Jim Hume, head of the company's detectives, and about as smart a dick as the West ever knew. It was Hume who'd got hold of the man who'd trapped Stiles. "All I'm asking you to do is put your name on that paper. You can write, can't you?"

"Sure I can, but I ain't gonna. Quick as I put my name on that paper you'd have me headed for Yuma with the rest of 'em. I ain't that dumb."

"I could have you clapped in jail for obstructing—"

"Go ahead! See what that gets you. You put me in front of any Grand Jury, mister, an' I'll deny the whole works. You fooled me once but you ain't doin' it again."

Hume nodded to one of his men and Billy was taken outside.

"As things stand right now," Colonel Randolph

said, "Alvord would laugh us out of court if we tried for a conviction. What you really want, and I can say the same for the railroad, is to get back the money."

One of the other men declared, "Dunlap's word, by itself, wouldn't carry no weight on a horse-high stack of prayerbooks. Stiles' confession, even if signed, could be shown as incompetent. Grover's testimony regarding what he got from that swamper would not be admissible as evidence. If we could find that swamper—"

"Not a chance," Hume sighed. "He got clean out of the country. Our best hope is Mossman—"

"We can't wait on Mossman," Colonel Randolph answered sharply. "Your Company, Hume, has threatened to deprive this region of express service—"

"I know," Hume said. "That's a large amount of money to have to lose in one chunk. You can't blame the Company; they've got to make a living too, you know. We stand to lose a hundred thousand on this case already. And it isn't only the money; there were a lot of valuable papers lost."

"I think," Randolph said, "there's no doubt Burt Alvord planned this steal. And I believe you gentlemen share my conviction that only Burt Alvord knows what has become of the loot; less, of course, the pittance he doled out to the rest of them. Why not make a deal with him?"

"I've already tried that," Hume said drily. "I offered to drop all charges if he'd return the gold and the papers."

"He refused?"

"Wouldn't even admit he knew what I was talking about."

One of the railroad dicks said, "Why not offer him a part of it to give back the rest?"

Hume shook his head. "We're dealing with a man who knows how to think and who has, moreover, worked long enough on the side of the law to sidestep any traps we might lay for him. Our only chance, as I see it, still revolves on Billy Stiles. He's in damned poor repute around here at the moment, practically a pariah. I happened to be in a saloon the other night when Stiles came in. In less than two minutes there was no one left in the place but him, myself and the barkeep."

"Might have been of more use if we'd locked him up."

"I don't think so. He's had a pretty good taste now of what folks think of him for going back on his friends. If we can get him to go visit Alvord maybe he could learn what Burt has done with the loot. I'll admit it's not likely but, if Alvord still refused him the share he thinks he's got coming, it might enrage Stiles enough that he would go into court and tell his story. It might just possibly get Alvord a stiff jail term. Then, if we offered Burt complete immunity—"

"It's worth a try," Randolph nodded. "Go ahead and put it up to him. Remind him of the reward we're offering for recovery of the gold. I think perhaps you should tell him also that if he doesn't get anywhere with Alvord, and still refuses to sign his confession, we'll have no alternative but to treat him the same as the rest of them."

Stiles was called in and the boss of the Wells Fargo investigators said, "It looks as though I've done all I can for you, Billy. You haven't given the cooperation we were led to expect from you. My colleagues in this matter think you ought to be in jail. As they point out, you blew the safes; you're the man who actually grabbed the swag. You've admitted that much and these gentlemen see no reason why you should not be given the full penalty of the law. But if you'll turn up the gold—"

"Fat chance I've got of doin' that," Stiles muttered.

"You may have a lot better chance than you imagine," Hume declared. "According to your version, when the loot was divided you and the others were fobbed off with a few hundred apiece. In your boots I would feel that I'd been gypped and gypped badly. Why don't you drop round and have a talk with Burt Alvord—"

"What the hell good would that do?"

"He knows you've made a statement. He knows you haven't signed it."

"Yeah," Stiles said, eyes glinting; and the detective pointed out: "That was gold in those bags, not silver, Billy. If you'd only grabbed three thousand would we be spending all these months trying to find it? Would we offer a reward which totaled more than we'd lost? He's played you boys for a bunch of damned fools. Now here's our proposition: If you don't turn up that gold or sign the confession you have made inside the next seven days, you're going to Yuma with the rest of them. But get us back that gold and those papers and I'll see that you get the full reward and perhaps a little something extra."

"Would that 'extra' cover a trip to Honduras?"

Hume said thoughtfully, "I don't see why it shouldn't. Down there you could live like a king on what we'd give you."

"All right," Stiles growled, "I'll take a whack at it. But don't look for no miracles. I prob'ly won't get no place with him."

"You've got a whole week. And half a lifetime in Yuma if you don't pull it off."

Stiles accordingly showed up at the Tombstone jail the next morning and, passed in on Hume's authority, spent two hours talking with Alvord. The guard, on orders, remained at the end of the corridor where he had the visitor under surveillance but was unable to overhear what they were saying except for occasional snatches which appeared to bear out Stiles' purpose in being there.

The following noon he dropped round again.

Jailer Braven, in the outer office, put aside his paper and, with a yawn, leaned back in his chair and stretched. "How's it going?" he asked affably. "You want to tackle him again?"

"We didn't get no place yesterday," Stiles grumbled. Then, curiously looking around, he said, "Where's all your gunhawks, George?"

"Regular boys has gone out to eat. The extras went off with the sheriff after—"

"Then suppose," snapped Stiles, "you just hand me them keys!" Like a flash he yanked a gun from his pocket and rammed the snout of it into Braven's stomach.

The surprised jailer turned pale. "Don't be a fool, Bill—"

"You'll find out if I'm foolin'—Get up off your prat an' go unlock them cells!"

The blazing look of Stiles' eyes convinced Braven that to hesitate longer would be to get himself killed without purpose. He reluctantly got up, fetched his keys off the hook and, watchfully followed by the man with the gun, opened the door to the cell block. "Watch your step," Stiles cautioned. "You're a baked duck, George, if you try any tricks."

Under Stiles' glittering eyes Braven unlocked Alvord's cell. "I'll be right with you," Alvord chuckled. "Turn 'em all out while you're at it."

He came back from the office buckling on his gun belts and with a couple of extras looped over his left arm. One of these he passed to Matt Berts, then looked with surprise to where Downing, beyond his cell's open door, still remained on his bunk. "What's the matter, Bill? Ain't you comin'?" Burt called.

"No, thanks," Downing answered. "I'm comfortable right here."

Alvord frowned at him a moment. "Have you lost your mind?"

"You're a goddam fool if you go out of here with Stiles, Burt—that little floppy-jawed bastard would doublecross his own kinfolks if he saw half a chance of turning up an extra buck! How do you know when you step outa that door you won't be walkin' slapbang into a bunch of Wells Fargo gunhands?"

"Well, I don't," Burt admitted, "but—"

"Then go ahead, if you're bound to, but don't expect me to go with you. I know when I'm well off, by God, an' I'm not takin' any more chances on Stiles."

Stiles came back up the corridor just then, prodding Braven along with the snout of his pistol. "You turned 'em all loose?" Alvord asked him.

"Sure—they've sloped out the side door; all but that big baboon at the end there."

"Here, give me the keys an' I'll let him out, too. What we want," Alvord said, "is enough confusion to sidetrack attention an' this *mozo* will come nearer doin' that than anyone."

He unlocked Chacon's cell and tossed him the gunbelt he had fetched for Bill Downing. He watched while the Mexican strapped it around him with a mumbled, "*Gracias, senor*," and then he said to Stiles: "Ed outside with my horses?"

"He oughta be, time we get out there."

"Let's go then," Burt growled; but in the office as they were helping themselves to the sheriff's Winchesters Matt Berts asked, with a glance at gaunt Chacon, "We takin' that feller?"

"He can ride the bronc I was figurin' to give Downing."

"I'll go first then," Berts said, and ducked out the front door.

As the others were crossing the office to follow, Braven made a grab at a gun and Stiles shot him. He had fired from the hip and the bullet, going into the jailer's leg, knocked him sprawling. Stiles was turning back to finish him when Alvord caught him by the shoulder. "What the hell do you think you're tryin' to do now?" With an angry scowl he sent him spinning toward the door.

EIGHTEEN

Burt Mossman

Alvord, coming out of Cochise County's two-storied red brick courthouse into the full bright smash of the overhead sun, was astonished to find the dusty street deserted. It seemed incredible Stiles' shot had not fetched the whole town running. He knuckled the white glare from his eyes and looked again, but it was so. No faces peered from the windows of those houses flanking the north side of Tough Nut; no one ran from the residences hemming the courthouse east and west. It was the damnedest jailbreak Burt has ever heard of but he was not one to quarrel with any gifts from Providence.

Hurrying around to the rear they found the man with their horses and, as they swung into the waiting saddles, Alvord said: "Where's Matt?"

"He piled aboard your bay gelding and struck off toward Benson."

Burt shook his head and Chacon, reining his openmouthed mount back onto its haunches, curbed his impatience with a look of polite enquiry. Stiles, not so polite, cried nervously: "For Christ's sake, let's not pick any daisies!"

"I think," Alvord said, "we better hit for the border," and Chacon nodded.

Stiles looked astounded. "My God, Burt—the loot! You ain't fixin' to leave it here, are you?"

Burt, slanching him a grinning glance, said "Sure," and kicked his pony into a run.

By the time the alarm was sounded—fully thirty minutes later—there was no way of being certain which direction the fugitives had taken. People were questioned along both sides of the street but no one had any suggestions to offer and the ground did not yield any promising tracks. Braven told what he knew, which was no help whatever, and an hour after the jail had been emptied—Downing thought perhaps they had struck out for Canada—several groups of mounted men turned out to scour the country—discreetly.

A lot of people thought the whole deal smelt fishy; others complained of criminal negligence. Del Lewis blamed Wells Fargo and the Express Company doubled the rewards and put every man they could spare on the case. About half of these took up the search while the rest, reenforced by dicks from the railroad, maintained constant vigilance lest Alvord slip back to dig up his cache. The Governor was appealed to and the bounty money mounted. There was twelve thousand dollars on Chacon's head alone and even more on Alvord's. Captain Mossman moved his

Ranger headquarters to Bisbee and the wires hummed but the fugitives remained at large.

Six months after the jailbreak Puddin Taylor, returning from town with a wagonload of groceries, knocked on the ranch house door and handed Bella a letter with a foreign looking stamp. "Figured mebbe," he said, "you wouldn't want this knowed about."

Bella's cheeks turned pale but her eyes silently thanked him. The continual tug between heart and mind since Alvord's departure had left its mark in her matured appearance; she had fought her silent battle during the lonely hours of sleepless nights and had no squeamish regrets for the ideals she had sacrificed. She was a woman in love and was prepared to cherish it no matter what damning facts came to light. She knew her love was returned and that was all that mattered.

"I expect," Taylor said, "he's havin' pretty tough sleddin' but they won't ketch him, you mark my words. An' while we're talkin' there's somethin' I been meanin' to tell you, ma'am. That day you went off to meet Kraitch in Tombstone, a certain party pulled in here not so long after you'd left. He had a couple of mighty heavy lookin' nosebags on his saddle an', if you ketch what I mean, I think he'd fetched 'em out here to take care of that note Kraitch was holdin' over you. I ain't mentioned this to nobody. I just reckoned you'd like to know."

He didn't wait for any thanks but limped back to his wagon in the haste of a strong man embarrassed by sentiment.

Bella went into the house and tore open her letter, eyes blurring as she read the brief message scrawled in pencil:

> I think of you a lot. I made a bad mistake pullin out of there like I done an I won't hold you to your promise. A man on the dodge ain't got no right to a woman.

It was signed quite simply: Burt Alvird.

And the months rolled by.

Chacon was up to his old tricks again and, in one sweeping raid across the International Line, drove as far north as Jerome where they held up a gambling house, murdered two prospectors, thundered into a sheep camp, killed two shearers and stuck up a stagecoach before retiring once again into the safety of the Sierra Madres. Just prior to this, and shortly after escaping from Tombstone where he'd been taken to be hanged, he'd led a daylight raid into Morenci, sacked the general store and cut Becker, the proprietor, into ribbons with a hide knife, packed his mules with plunder and gone larruping up the canyon. But the Graham County sheriff had been right on his heels. He ran the bandits into a box canyon and a considerable amount of lead was exchanged although no one seemed to have been very much hurt. The outlaws could not escape with their horses unless they came through the egress guarded by the posse. They could, however, by abandoning their horses, climb out of the trap once darkness descended. One of Birchfield's Mexican deputies who had known Chacon south of the border thought he might be able to talk the fellow into surrendering, but as soon as he rode into sight Chacon shot him. Another battle was joined and, during the night, most of the outlaws vanished into the hills. Chacon, badly wounded, was captured the next morning, but he broke jail again, regathered his gang and swept shooting and yelling through the outskirts of Phoenix.

Governor Murphy, under pressure from all sides, summoned his Ranger boss, Mossman. "Now see here," he said grimly, "I know Wells Fargo and the Southern Pacific are raising hell about Alvord but this hombre Chacon is a public menace! What are you doing about catching him?"

Mossman said he was doing all he could within the law; that he had finally succeeded in negotiating an unofficial working agreement with Col. Emilio Kosterlitzky, head of the Mexican Rurales; that, in addition, he had formed a kind of secret police among the rowdy element of Bisbee and was hoping, through this organization, to locate Alvord's half-brother in Mexico. He had every reason to suppose this fellow would know where Burt was holed up.

"But it's Chacon I want!" The Governor pounded the table. "All Alvord's done is rob a corporation—this fellow Chacon is looting the whole Territory! Do you realize he's killed twenty-nine American citizens? I want that butcher caught!"

"I understand," Mossman nodded, "but Burt Alvord's the answer. You've had a lot of complaints about me not catching Alvord; the truth of the matter is I haven't even tried. And the reason I haven't tried is because I need Alvord to help me catch Chacon. The sheriffs of Cochise and Santa Cruz counties are the two biggest reasons I haven't done it already—they've got no blinkety-blank business chasing down into Mexico after the reward on Alvord's scalp but they've done it time and again. We can't complain about Chacon while they're leading armed invasions into Mexico in defiance of every statute on the books! You don't see them dashing down there trying to find Chacon!"

"What makes you think Burt Alvord will help you?"

"He won't as things stand. We've got to be prepared to make some pretty large concessions.

Now I've discovered through certain of my connections that Alvord's anxious to come in and I believe, if you would guarantee him a fair trial—"

"Of course he'll have a fair trial!"

"—and guarantee that if he helps me land Chacon you'll do your best to get him off lightly."

"What makes you think he can help you?"

"I'm told he knows where Chacon's hideout is and has, upon occasion, actually used it himself when Lewis and those bounty-hunters got too close upon his heels."

"Will he turn over the loot he took off that train?"

"I think, originally, he would have; I think by this time, however, he probably figures he's earned it. I've talked to Judge Barnes about him and the Judge says he'll do what he can for Burt too in the event this works out. There's another reason why I feel the man may want to come in. He was wounded several months ago in a brush with one of those sheriff's posses; shot through the wrist, I hear. The wound won't heal and I imagine it's pretty painful; he's bound to know it needs a doctor's attention. If gangrene sets in he's apt to lose the whole arm."

"Very well," Murphy said. "This Territory can afford to forgive a man considerable if he helps bring about the arrest of that butcher, Chacon. You may tell him we'll stand behind him."

From Judge Barnes, Mossman secured a letter stating very clearly that in return for his help with Chacon he could expect the best efforts of the Governor, the Judge and the Captain of the Rangers. Most of the witnesses against him, the letter explained, were dead, jailed or gone from the country. His chances of acquittal were excellent; at the worst he could expect but a very light sentence—if he cared to cooperate. That, in addition, the Judge was prepared to defend him free of charge.

"You're taking a terrible risk," Barnes said as he handed Mossman the letter. "The man's bound to be desperate. All that chasing Del Lewis and Tom Turner have been giving him must have Alvord pretty well stirred up and on edge—not to mention the cutthroats he may have around him. And if he's in the Sierra Madres you might run into Chacon's main bunch. You're intending to go alone?"

"Of course," Mossman nodded. "I'd never get to Alvord any other way."

"You may have to employ that twisty Stiles before you're done with this. Near as I been able to learn he's the only one around here who knows where Alvord's half-brother's at."

Captain Mossman smiled grimly. Incensed at the way Stiles had been coddled prior to the jailbreak at Tombstone his men had been making things hot for Stiles every time the man slipped back over the border. "That may hold me up awhile if you're right. At the moment he's hiding in the Papago Desert, chased on this side by my men and on the other by Kosterlitzky's."

To complicate things still further, just as Mossman was about to get things lined up and had discovered through his secret service that Alvord's half-brother was down in Sonora running a big engine used to force water up to the Minas Prietas smelter, President McKinley's assassination threw politics into a turmoil. All Territorial officials, from the Governor straight down through the chief of the Rangers, were compelled by custom to tender their resignations.

But Mossman did not give up his plans for catching Chacon. He was still holding a commission as Deputy United States Marshal. Chacon's stagecoach robberies had interfered with the mails so he could still go after him on that charge. Some of the men Mossman's Rangers had convicted and sent to prison had powerful friends and these had never been more active in trying to have him ousted; the partisan press had also been hounding him, charging him and his service with all manner of laxness, officiousness, favoritism and flagrant disregard for the limitations of his office. To all of these he had turned a deaf ear; but now, with his resignation in, he was in a frame of mind to consider desperate measures in his efforts to bring Chacon to justice.

At Nogales he boarded a southbound train and, at Tores, took the branch run to Minas Prietas. The manager of the smelter was an Englishman and after shooting the breeze for about a quarter of an hour Mossman decided to take him into his confidence. This gentleman said, if Mossman insisted, he would reluctantly provide him with a suitable number of mules to insure transportation for the trip back into the hills to the place where Alvord's relation was running the steam pump. It was twenty-four miles, he said, through difficult country, and he strongly advised Mossman not to attempt it.

But Mossman had no intention of being turned back now. All his life he'd been facing grave risks and doing impossible things. Showing the manager a wintry smile, he said: "Have your outfit here first thing in the morning."

NINETEEN

Mexican Gallop

Even before the fugitives had gone a dozen miles Alvord heartily regretted the whimsical impulse which had caused him to liberate Augustin Chacon. It had seemed at the time an inspired bit of business to have so dread an outlaw sharing their flight; it was obvious Chacon's presence would imbue any pursuit with a considerable amount of caution and, once they had put the border markers behind them, common gratitude should incline the man toward equipping Stiles and Alvord with a suitable hideout. But Burt had reckoned without knowledge of Chacon's character. They had hardly gotten out of sight of Tombstone before the black-browed bandit was suggesting they stick up the bank at Bisbee.

Mexican fancy had built around the man a legend of glamour in the Robin Hood pattern which was without any vestige of foundation in fact. Chacon was practically a moron with the cunning of a wolf, and with all the social grace and morals of one also. He was totally without fear and activated almost entirely by instinct and impulse. When Alvord vetoed the suggested

Bisbee foray the bandit went into a brooding sulk which lasted halfway to the border.

Alvord rode with cold chills running up and down his spine every time that brush or gullies forced the man to drop behind him. Before they crossed the line he had silently resolved to part company with the Mexican at the earliest opportunity.

Twice they sighted lone ranch hands in the distance and on each occasion Chacon, with his bunch-of-banana fingers lovingly wrapped around his gun butt, had plaintively proposed they go and "ventilate the bastard."

They were two miles south of Naco and getting into the Mexican foothills when Chacon set his rearing horse on its haunches. "*Despensame, senors*," he said in his most polite fashion, "but what do you do after this, eh?"

"Haven't given it a thought," Alvord said without truth.

"Then I suggest we fill our bellies while the *senors* commune with the future. A cantina I know of is but a few *metros* from this place."

"Any women?" Stiles inquired with a wink, and Chacon gave him a very wide grin.

"*Si, mucho*," he nodded. "Is but around that next hill and the sun is low. I show you—come!"

It was plain when they reached the cantina that the tall mustachioed bandit boss was a man who commanded much respect in these parts. Nothing was considered too good for him and the fugitives enjoyed an excellent supper heavily garnished with chile and copious draughts of warm beer. When nothing remained to be eaten Chacon said, "I have been doing much thinking, *amigos*. In my camp I have many followers—an army, no less; but alas these so-great fighters have heads like the burro—*no bueno por nada*."

He showed his broad teeth in a grin of contempt and Alvord, sensing what was coming, tried to catch Stiles' eyes but Billy, at the moment, was much too taken up with admiring the curves of the magnificent animal who had fetched in their suppers, a scantily-clad sixteen-year-old answering to the name of Conchita.

Alvord kicked Stiles under the table. Stiles swung round with a growl of protest. Alvord said: "Pay attention to the general. He's thinking of making you a strawboss in his outfit."

Chacon nodded. "That is so," he declared. "I make you *capitans*. *Sta bueno*, no?"

"I dunno," Stiles said. "That calico" —and he jerked his head at Conchita who was hugging her knees on a stool by the bar's end—"go with the job?"

Chacon grinned. "*Seguro si*," he said, slapping Stiles on the back. "Plenty of womens, plenty *tequila, muchos pesos*!"

Stiles grinned too. "Conchita! *Andale— pronto*!" he called and, when she came over to their table, "*Mi bandida*!" he laughed, and pulled her onto his knee.

Chacon, who'd been watching Alvord out of the corners of his narrowed eyes, said abruptly: "You don't like for be my *capitan*, maybe?"

"Well," Burt answered, very careful with his words, "I'd kind of like to think it over—"

"*Seguro*," Chacon dragged a massive timepiece from his pocket. He shook it like a bottle, held it to his ear and finally laid it on the table. "I give you two minutes. Go ahead."

Alvord sent his glance around a ring of scowling faces. "How much choice you giving me?"

"You be *capitan* or I put you against adobe wall."

Alvord cocked his muscles to come erect in a hurry. Grinning widely at the outlaw he addressed Stiles casually in English. "Be ready to run for it when I shove over this table."

Chacon's teeth gleamed behind his ragged mustache. He said, also in English: "When you push over the table you are dead mans, *gringo*."

"I guess," Burt sighed, "we'll leave the table where it is."

Thus, for a briefly hectic while, Burt Alvord and Augustin Chacon rode the trails in double harness. In spectacular raids they sacked several *haciendas* and made fools of the Rurales. Chacon helped Burt elude the Express Company's agents and the hard-riding posses thrown against him by the sheriffs of Santa Cruz and Cochise counties, revealing many a cunning hideout among the towering Sierra Madres. When the Governor of Sonora ordered out his Palace Guards it was Augustin Chacon who kept Burt out of the reach of their hungry rifles. To all outward appearances they were the best of *buen amigos*—real *compadres* of the saddle; underneath this show neither one of them trusted the other any farther than he could have thrown him.

It was a nerve-racking business and Burt was damned well fed up with it but Chacon's vigilance never slackened. It pleased his ego to have the *gringo* taking his orders and he was crafty enough to make sure Alvord had no real chance to get away from him. Stiles, on the other hand, was given the run of the camp and one day, while Burt was taking a cautious bath about six inches from his bone-handled pistols, Stiles came sauntering over to the near side of the creek and, with the abused look he affected on such occasions, prepared to reopen the discussion of Burt's loot.

In a voice fairly drooling self-pity he declared, "It's a damn sorry thing when a man's own friends go back on him, Burt. It ain't that I care about Downing or Berts—they got just what they asked for, the way I look at it. But you an' me's been friends for a helluva long time an' it don't seem right you should hog all that gold when it was me in the first place that figured out how to grab it."

Burt's lip corners tightened but he lathered his chest without bothering to answer.

"The way I look at it," Stiles pressed, "you made enough freezin' the rest out to give me my full share. Look at it this way. If it hadn't been for me you'd still be penned up in Tombstone, or mebbe Yuma by this time. I took a helluva lot of risk bustin' you outa that jail an' it's only right you should consider that fact."

"You got me out of that jail for one of two reasons," Burt said grimly. "Either to give them Wells Fargo dicks a chance to catch me diggin' up the stuff or else in the hope I would be damn fool enough to cut you in deeper. You was wrong on both counts."

Stiles eyed him slanchways. "You'd be in bad way if I was to tell this guy Chacon you got the bulk of eighty thousand stashed away across the line an' another fourteen thousand bucks in bounty on your—"

He didn't stop to finish. Burt was already striding toward his guns and the look of his unshaved face scared Stiles spitless. He bolted for his horse and fled the camp in fear of his life.

Three days later, during a raid on a ranch south of Agua Prieta, Alvord himself slipped his picket

218

pin and got away into the nearby mountains. All night he played hide and seek with Chacon's horsemen but when the sun came up bright and red the next morning Paludo's cutthroats were gone.

During the next several months he led a precarious existence, frequently under fire and relentlessly hounded by the incursions of sheriffs' posses and the private forays of individual bounty hunters in addition to the continuing efforts of Wells Fargo and the railroad whose agents, anxious to track down the loot he had hidden, still hoped to get their hands on him. The Rurales, too, were still after him and he was forced to shift bases time and again. He lived during those days mainly on rabbits and gophers though he was twice compelled to eat snake meat when so closely pressed he dared not discharge either pistol or rifle. Many times he broke into isolated stores to get a little variety into his diet and to replenish his dwindling stocks of ammunition. Once, when he was particularly desperate, he robbed a store in broad daylight; but mostly he did all he could to stay hidden, knowing that every man's hand was against him.

Gaunt and unshaven he was a wild looking figure in the brush-clawed clothing that looked sizes too big for his emaciated frame. He more resembled some weatherbeaten scarecrow than a flesh and blood man for whom the combined rewards now totaled $15,000.

Many times he was forced to use Chacon's own hideouts, even at the risk of being recaptured by Paludo; once he was driven straight into the bandit's main stronghold. This was the occasion on which Del Lewis' deputies almost caught him; he did manage to get clear of them but they put one slug clean through his right wrist and it was this which finally brought him back to Chacon.

The Hairy One was across the border on one of his raids but there were a number of camp followers holding down the place and one of these bound the wound up with herbs; and Burt lit out before Chacon returned.

It was this experience which had caused him to write Bella.

Countless times since his escape into Mexico he had mercilessly examined the unsatisfactory present and cast up the probable value of the future in the light of his past activities without discovering much foundation on which to predicate hope of security.

Circumstances had certainly been ripe for his follies but he did not imagine these had maneuvered him into them. He had made his own choices and they had mostly been bad ones, yet he saw very clearly that, given another chance, he would still have come to this same desperate pass. He knew his limitations. He did not feel he had the right to ask any decent woman—and surely Bella least of all—to share the price he must pay to hang onto that treasure. For there was the crux of the whole sorry business. He could give the loot up but he was damned if he was going to.

There was no use trying to kid himself at this stage. Call it pride, call it bullheaded stubbornness, but he was determined to hang onto that gold at any cost. He had wondered many times if this thing he felt for Bella was what the world described as love—if he could make her a good husband, a good father for her children; for she would want kids just as he did. And he couldn't honestly answer. He knew only that he wanted her as he had never wanted another woman; he believed he could make her happy but the question was for *how long?*

He had achieved a reputation for being the fastest man with a gun on record, so fast and so deadly able to call his shots no man save Cowboy Bill had dared call him. It was his greatest accomplishment, his most tangible asset, but hardly a thing to guarantee continued bliss in double harness. The world was filled with the kind of damned fools who would do anything at all to get their names into the headlines. He had never worried about such people, but a woman would.

221

They could go somewhere else—Honduras or Canada—and he could change his name, but would that be enough? Could any man truly cut loose of his past or completely bury the talents he'd been born with?

These were things Burt Alvord couldn't answer. But these were some of the things which had finally decided him to send that brief note to Bella.

Summer had claimed the desert in grim earnest. From dawn till dark the sun's blazing disc swam through the brassy skies. Day after insufferable day its blazing heat and furnace breath seared the vegetation and beat through tin and tar-paper roofs till eyeballs burned and things caught without water dropped their bones in the blistering sands, their fried meat prey to the buzzards and coyotes. Even the trees in the mountains turned brown and stream after stream was sucked out of existence.

Burt Alvord survived but all the laughter went out of him.

When the fall winds blew the trapped heat off the desert he came down from the crags, a shrunken caricature of the boisterous scoffer who had once marshaled Willcox. He looked like a wild man on a bag of bones when he rode into one of Chacon's foothills rendezvous about a two days' ride from Minas Prietas. Five of Chacon's bravos were holed up in the stone hut and spilled out like ants from a burning log at the sound of his horse's hoofs on the trail.

Five months ago he'd have laughed at their ludicrous expressions of recognition. As it was he said nothing till one of the group, mouthing blasphemies, made a grab at his pistol.

"Stop!" Alvord croaked through fever-cracked lips. "There's room enough here for—" But the bastard had his gun clear and when its barrel swung level Alvord, cursing, killed him. The others backed off with their hands up, shaking, their eyes like burnt marbles threatening to leap from their sockets.

Alvord swung down and limped into the shack. "Take care of my horse," he flung over his shoulder, "and drag that carrion off someplace an' bury it."

Fear was the only thing they would answer to and they were as frightened of Burt as they'd have been of the devil.

It took him three solid weeks to get over that summer and even then he was like a man dragged through a knothole. His wrist wouldn't heal; it turned him savagely irascible and sometimes he thought he was about to go crazy. It was on one of those days that, with a rifle held loosely in the crook of his left arm, he stepped out of the shack and saw a strange rider rounding the bend of the trail.

• • •

The man came straight on, both paws clasped on the pommel, letting the horse pick its way. If he packed any artillery—and presumably he did—at least he was careful to keep his hands plumb away from it. He was a well-fed good-looking sort of a jasper in store clothes with the brim of his Stet hat tugged low to shade his eyes. When he'd got to within twenty feet Burt called, "Hold it!" and watched the fellow stop his horse with his knees.

An experienced rider. And he was armed, all right, and showed the coldest pair of eyes Burt had ever looked into. "I presume," he said casually, "I'm talking to Burt Alvord?"

"You're takin' a hell of a lot for granted!"

"I've some pictures of you in my office. I'm Cap Mossman of the Arizona Rangers."

"Glad to know you," Alvord scoffed. "I'm Colonel Randolph of the Southern Pacific."

"Perhaps," the stranger suggested with a tight-lipped smile, "you'd like to look over my—"

"Move them hands an' you're a cooked goose, mister!"

Through a tightening stillness the two men locked eyes. Alvord growled, suddenly convinced, "Some of them silk tiles in Arizona is goin' to look plumb foolish when they find out Burt Alvord's holdin' you over here for ransom." He drew a ragged breath. "You crazy son of a

224

bitch, I just got them goddam sheriffs off my tail! Where's the rest of your pussyfootin' outfit?"

Mossman's cheeks paled a little but his eyes never wavered. "Taking care of their regular work I imagine. Mr. Alvord, I've come to see you as a friend—"

"Did you bring along a string of spools for me to play with?"

"No, but I've fetched you a letter from Judge Barnes which I think you ought to read because it's of considerable importance to you. I give you my word this is no kind of trap."

Alvord stared for a couple of moments and Mossman said persuasively, "I've also talked with Bella Norton and I bring you news from her—"

"What news?" Alvord's voice was a rasp.

"She asked me to tell you that she's sold her ranch and is ready to join you in a new start—"

"I've got a fat chance of that!"

"You have a very good chance, as you will see if you care to read Barnes' letter. She wants you to know she's still waiting and will go with you anyplace whenever you care to come after her."

Alvord's eyes shone like bits of polished glass. "Where's this letter?"

"Right here in my coat pocket. You can see the top of it sticking out if you'll look—and I wish you'd tell those hombres of yours to point their rifles in some other direction. I'm not up to any tricks."

Alvord barked a gruff order to Chacon's riff-raff in Spanish. "Let's see the letter. If you ain't tellin' the truth you're goin' to damn soon regret it."

Mossman waited till the rifles had disappeared behind the shack's gun slots, then he got off his horse and handed Alvord the letter.

Burt read it in silence. After he'd finished he read it over again and stood scowling awhile, obviously turning something over in his mind. "What do you want me to do?" he said finally.

"First of all I'd like to get a bite to eat if you can spare it. And I don't think we'd better talk in front of those ruffians—one of them might know enough English to catch the drift."

"All right. There's a sheep camp down this trail a piece. We'll eat there. Leave your horse."

He shouted another order to the men in the hut and then, as they set off down the trail, he said with a glance at Mossman's fancy pistol, "You better hide that gun. Some of these *mozos* might take a fancy to it."

"This gun stays right where it's at," Mossman told him.

"All right. You want to nab Chacon. Barnes says you fellers are willin' to help straighten me out. What have I got to do for it?"

"Put me where I can get hold of Chacon. It'll have to be someplace close to the border."

Alvord walked a few yards in silence. "I don't

suppose I owe that snake anything. Still, it kind of goes against the grain—"

"The man's a cold-blooded killer!"

"You're right about that."

"Then don't be a bigger fool than you have already."

"It ain't goin' to be easy," Alvord said, mighty thoughtful.

"What about Greene's race horses—why not sic him after them? They're just across the line on the Arizona side. Tell him you've got a friend that's just broken jail who knows all about those *caballos* and—"

"It might work," Burt said dubiously. "But you'd have to get Stiles to act as go-between and that won't be easy either. You'll have to offer him something pretty temptin' to get him to come within a mile of me or Chacon; and I ain't too anxious to get near Chacon myself. He's been huntin' me off an' on for a year."

"I'll take care of Stiles. You can introduce me to Chacon as the ranny that's busted jail; the gent that knows about the horses and a surefire way of getting clear with them. And here's what I'll do: As soon as I've got Chacon under wraps you give yourself up and I will go to bat for you. In fact I'll do more than that; I'll see that you and Stiles get all the rewards out for him. Is that a deal?"

Alvord nodded. "I'll send you word soon's we get it fixed up."

TWENTY

Alvord Rides

Back in Arizona Captain Mossman found that Major Brodie, formerly of the Rough Riders, had been installed as Governor by appointment of Teddy Roosevelt. Mossman's resignation was in but thus far had not been acted upon and so, while he was waiting for his head to hit the basket, he sent word via his undercover spies that he would welcome a visit from Stiles under a safe-conduct guarantee. Stiles came in and was quietly sworn in as a Ranger and assigned to the border with special orders. "You help Burt Alvord and me pull this off and we'll overlook what you've done in the past. And as an extra inducement I will see that you get half of all the rewards offered for Chacon."

Stiles disappeared into the desert. A few weeks later Mossman received a friendly letter from Governor Brodie asking him to stay on as boss factotum of the Rangers until he could select a suitable successor. This put Cap in a better frame of mind for, by this time, he was determined to bring Chacon to justice regardless.

But the Ranger captain's enemies among the crooks and politicians were doing everything in their power to force the new man at Phoenix to oust him. They bombarded Brodie with letters and telegrams, brought pressure to bear from every direction and, when he refused to be bluffed or intimidated, they went after Mossman directly. Gunmen were hired to assassinate him but the boss Ranger proved to have more lives than a cat. So they tried their hands at framing him and, while they didn't actually manage to trap him, stirred up enough adverse publicity that a petition was circulated calling on Brodie to relieve Cap of his office as head of the Territorial police force.

Great multitudes of people began to "take pen in hand" and, while the uproar was at its loudest, Mossman in a fit of anger wrote the Governor himself. And was informed his resignation would be effective as of the final day in August.

Counting the days in Bisbee, Mossman paced his office in a lather of impatience. From the start he'd been against doing business with a man of Stiles' caliber and had only agreed to do so because of Alvord's insistence. Chacon and Stiles, Alvord said, were already acquainted and the Mexican would be less likely to be suspicious with Stiles in the role of go-between.

Perhaps Burt was right but when the first of September came whistling in Mossman still had not had any word from Stiles. The new chief of Rangers—another Rough Rider—came down from the Capitol and was duly installed. But Mossman still held his commission as Deputy U. S. Marshal and he was still determined to deliver Paludo. He moved across to the hotel and the next afternoon he got the word he'd been waiting for.

Stiles fetched it himself, declaring Chacon had risen to the bait like a shark scenting blood.

Alvord, after Mossman had left him, remained in a cloud plowing mood for several days, bemused with the visions conjured by Barnes' letter and the knowledge that Bella still cared and was waiting. Bar 6 had meant a great deal to Norton's daughter and the fact that she could sell it in order to hold herself ready to rejoin him at a moment's notice left Burt feeling pretty damned humble.

He was grateful, too, that such important personages as Murphy, Judge Barnes and the boss of the Rangers should be willing to back him in a chance to start over, though he was not deceived by such apparent generosity into imagining they felt any personal regard for him. Mossman's remarks had made the facts plain on that score. They were helping him simply because they found it expedient; he represented the last possibility they could discover of nabbing Chacon. For five years hand-running the dread shadow of Paludo had hung like a blight across five hundred miles of border until finally his capture had become an obsession with them.

Burt wasn't quarreling with that. Nor with the probability that, once cleared, he'd be asked to haul his freight and get the hell out of Arizona and stay out. The blame for that lay with him and he assumed it; he'd had plenty of time during these months on the dodge to consider the depth of the rut he'd got into and to clearly understand that to make a fresh start he would have to go somewhere beyond the reach of past follies. And he felt, too, a considerable responsibility for the most of the more recent atrocities chalked up against Augustin Chacon. He had turned the butcher loose. It was entirely fitting and proper that he should be singled out to help run the man down.

Mossman's offer of half the reward money hadn't interested Burt in the slightest; what hesitation he had shown about accepting had been caused by realization of the factors involved. Trapping Paludo was no chore for weaklings and past associations could be as dangerous as helpful.

They could give his share of the rewards to Wells Fargo. He had agreed to Mossman's terms primarily because of Bella, because he had to have competent care for his wrist and because he still hoped to dig up that gold and get away with it. His desire for a fresh start was not coupled with visions of privation or drudgery.

But with the passing of days the inevitable reactions set in to undermine and tear down the fine castles he'd built on the floodtide of optimism. When five weeks had dragged past without further word from Mossman and no sign whatever of the loud-talking Stiles, Alvord watched the last shred of hope flake away.

He'd been a fool ever to think he'd get the chance to start over! When a steer quit the bunch he doomed himself to travel solo; same way with a wolf or that two-legged catamount, man. Fence-crawler! Maverick! Renegade! These were the names the world coined for such critters. Let who will sow the wind—but let him also reap the whirlwind!

Looking back on it now he couldn't see how Mossman's plan had stood much chance of succeeding anyway. Chacon, though in many respects having the mind of a kid, was far from being a total fool. Wily as a fox he was, and incomparably more deadly than the ringiest rattler. Bad as the man needed horses they'd been loco to dream he'd ever figure counting on *gringos* to help him get them. If Stiles had put it up to him he had probably by this time grabbed the whole lot and vanished like a whirled-apart dust devil. They might as well have tried to put salt on a sparrow's tail!

And there was Stiles to gum up the deal if everything else went according to schedule—

Stiles with his too-ready tendency to vacillate. Stiles, the hired gun who couldn't stay bought.

After the way he'd fled Chacon's camp that day it would take more than any mere splitting of rewards to fetch him face to face with Burt or that hairy Mexican again. And, even if it didn't, why the hell should Paludo trust him any more than he'd trust Burt Alvord? Just the memory of Paludo's baleful stare was enough to chase chills up the back of Burt's spine. *Bandido puro*—plumb cultus. A first class gent to stay a long ways away from.

And then, bright and early of a late fall morning with the air turning brisk as an ice-packed head of cabbage, Billy Stiles came around the bend of the trail and climbed off a big *grulla* just outside Burt's stone hut. The man's clothes were molded to him and shiny from long contact with the leathers of his saddle but his face wore a nervous smile. "I've got him hooked!"

"Fell for it, did he?"

"He'll meet you," Stiles said, "at your camp on the north side of San Jose Mountain, an' you're to go there alone. He gives you ten days to get there an' if you fetch anybody with you the whole deal is off."

"He say so?"

"Damn right he said so. He was keen enough about gettin' hold of Greene's horses but he couldn't see much sense in cuttin' you in on the business. He's still plenty sore about the way you run out on him. Don't take nobody with you; he's goin' to be watchin' that country through a pair of high-powered glasses. He said if you set any store on your health you'd better follow them instructions."

Burt right then would have followed almost anything. His spirits had hit high C again and he cooked Stiles up a hell of a breakfast, looking pleased as a kid with a new red wagon. He even cracked a bottle he'd been saving against snakebite.

Stiles cautiously broached the subject of rewards and Alvord said, tossing it over his shoulder, that for all of him Stiles could have the whole works.

Billy chewed for awhile, his glance gone bland as a goose-hair pillow; then he battened it down with the rest of the bottle and, fortified with this, he said: "All right, Burt—what's the wrinkle?"

Alvord stared, abruptly snorting. He pulled off the bandages and showed him. "I got to get this wrist fixed up —an' I mean quicklike."

Stiles looked and whistled. He still didn't see what the wound had to do with the rewards on Chacon's scalp but he wasn't inviting trouble by rattling off any string of questions.

"Well," he sighed, wiping his mouth on his sleeve, "I reckon I better be ridin'. You know where Carizzo Springs is, don't you? That's where me an' Mossman's going to meet you an' old Pop Whiskers. Don't be late an' don't fetch no one with you."

It was not until after Stiles had departed that Alvord began to wonder about the man's repeated warning not to take anybody with him to the rendezvous with Chacon. Why had Stiles been so insistent?

The more Burt pondered the less he liked it; and Stiles' patent hurry to cut short the visit did little to reassure him. Why the hell was Stiles acting so edgy?

Burt was sorely tempted to await the gang's return and take the four of them with him. He might have done it, too, had he seen any chance of depending on their loyalty; but they were Chacon's men and, in the event of any trouble, they'd be bound to side with Paludo.

There was too much at stake to risk tampering with the arrangements. If Stiles was fixed to pull any kind of fast one Burt would simply have to do the best that he was able and hope like hell his luck would pull him through.

He threw the gear on his gelding and struck off into the desert, heading north by east. He reckoned, without he ran into trouble going through some of these mountains, to get there in plenty of season; but there was always the chance his horse would break a leg or maybe suffer some other equally disastrous calamity, in which case he might be hard-pressed to make it. And there was always the danger of bandits to contend with when a man took a *pasear* across this part of Sonora. Every move a man made in Manyanner Land was likely to be threatened by unexpected hazards; and so, to be on the safe side, he moved right along. He sure hoped to hell he wasn't going to have to play tag with any of Del Lewis' posses.

Nor was he overlooking the possibility of an encounter with railroad or express company agents. Neither one of those outfits had yet completely relinquished hope of recovering the loot taken off the westbound flyer. This wasn't the season for streams to be in flood but there was always the chance, working through strange mountains, that a man would lose a day trying to get around some barrier shoved in his path by nature, an impassable gorge or blind canyon.

He was traveling light and for the first three days he kept right up with his schedule, but on the fourth he found himself forced to cross a really high range which he had not been through before. He aimed for what looked like a notch between the peaks but, when in late afternoon he came onto it, it was so choked with broken rock he could not get his horse through it.

Twisting around in the saddle he looked over his back-trail, at the tortuous maze of *barrancas*, *mesas* and *canones* he had traversed in reaching this place, and cursed like a mule skinner. It had taken him the best part of the day to get up here and, if he were compelled to go back, it meant the loss of another day—perhaps two, because he still had to find a way to reach the other side.

He considered the battered peaks. The one to his left towered five hundred feet above him; the one at his right did not seem quite as high but it looked very nearly solid stone and was obviously too steep to be scaled at this point by a man on a horse and there were at least four days of riding still ahead of him.

Stiles, of course, had not come this way but had struck out north by a little bit west in the direction of Nogales, traveling one of the troughs between these mountain ranges. Burt could have done that, too, swinging east toward Naco where the mountains were much lower—he could, that is, if he'd been willing to disregard the fifteen thousand offered for his pelt in bounty money. Stiles, by his tell of it, had been secretly made a Ranger and there'd been nothing posted on him but a measly five hundred dollars.

Burt sighed and, looking round him, swore again. He could not afford to turn back if there were any way of avoiding it. He calculated that north slope again and finally decided to tackle it. After twenty minutes of casting about he came upon the dim sign of what appeared at one time to have been a trail leading upward. Some kind of game had likely made it and he decided before he'd climbed a hundred feet it had probably been made by mountain goats. He was frequently forced to get off and lead his gelding and a couple of times it didn't look like even then they were going to make it; at one hundred and twenty-five feet the thing went into a series of switchbacks, long ones at first but gradually shortening as they climbed through the talus. The last brush fell away. Scoured sandstone appeared and the trail rose into the windy open. Bright sunlight and sky and the screech of the wind like claws tearing at them and nothing on either side but sheer space.

Some men might have paused to admire the majestic grandeur of the view spread out below them, but not Alvord. He felt about as cold as a man could get yet sweat made a shine on the backs of his fists and the parts of his face that were not stubbled with bristle gleamed as though oiled. He kept his eyes bleakly fixed between the ears of his gelding and both hands clamped to the horn of his saddle. Had he considered himself able he would have gotten off and crawled, but there wasn't any place to *get* off. The trail clung precariously to the surface of sheer rock, barely wide enough to afford the horse footing. Half the time Burt's right thigh was scraping the wall, and the times that it wasn't his other thigh was.

He was too scared even to curse.

And still they climbed, up and up, a few steps left, then a few to the right, but always and ever moving perilously higher with the shriek of the wind tearing round them like demons and doing its damnedest to buffet them off. It had snatched Burt's hat and whipped out his shirt tails and in its gusty clutch the whangstrings of his saddle were popping like bullets. And then abruptly, with no other warning than the increased ferocity of that hell-spawned gale, they came onto the top of the peak's craggy knob. An eagle's perch on the roof of the world. Twenty-eight feet of highly tenuous rock with nothing round about it but the howling turquoise sky.

The gelding groaned to a stop and stood there shaking and quaking while each slap of the wind threatened to sweep the quivering legs out from under them. Burt's mouth felt dry as the bed of that lake through which he had tracked the flight of the robbers. He wanted to get down, to crawl off this damned horse, but his hands were froze to the horn of the saddle. He didn't dare go back and there was nothing beyond the gelding's flared nostrils but eleven feet of buff rock and a leap into hell. The rest of the crag had broken away for thousands of feet straight down.

He finally forced himself to look to the right. One look was enough to last him a lifetime—there was absolutely nothing but space on that side, space stretching clean and blue to eternity.

And then his horse with a forlorn whinny started moving again, bearing left on gimpy hoofs whose shod clatter was snatched away in the wail of the wind. And Burt saw, leading west as though straight into the maw of the sun's red death, a narrow ledge of gray rock extending like a kind of swinging bridge to another and lesser peak perhaps a half a mile away.

It was scarcely more than four feet wide, a sort of ledge-like shelf skewered above space by long steel bars driven into the spine of a connecting ridge, the outer edges of them showing red with rust at frequent intervals. Burt understood then that this trail he had been following was not, after all, the work of mountain goats but a thing built by Spaniards perhaps a hundred years ago. This knowledge however did little to make the prospect of crossing it more endearing.

He had always had a horror of high places and abruptly shut his eyes lest these terrifying sights should cause him to become lightheaded and go spilling out of his saddle. But he was even more frightened not to know what was happening and jerked them open in wild alarm lest some sudden mistake on the part of his horse bring about the very thing he was trying so desperately to avoid.

It was the sort of thing a man experiences in nightmare and he was trembling like a leaf when the gelding stepped off the ledge's far side onto the comparable security of the lesser crag at the shelf's western terminal. This knob was wider and its slope much less precipitous yet he dared not stop with night so close upon them. This portion of the trail was no better than the other, narrower if anything and with all the signs of soon becoming impassable. Long slants of the descending switchbacks were heavy strewn with rubble and in some places, several times for as much as three feet, were so badly eroded the horse had to jump them. Each time this happened Burt felt sure the lathered gelding was going to lose his footing, though he somehow never did.

Dusk faded into full darkness and there was no place to stop. The wind whistled eerily around the shoulders of the turns and all they needed now, he thought, was a gully-washer or to come head-on into a mountain lion to land them squarely in joy street.

It took them two hours to get down into timber and Burt reckoned he had aged ten years in the process. The gelding stood on braced legs while Burt pulled the gear off him and he was still huddled there, shaking, when Burt without eating dropped into the sleep of utter exhaustion.

The sun, though invisible, was well into the heavens, gilding the tops of the hundred-foot pines, when he awoke the next morning to find the gelding still grazing some fifty yards away.

Burt whistled him over and got him ready for travel. There was still a little water in his canvas-wrapped canteen but, now that he'd lost his hat, no way in which he could share this with his horse. He could pour some out in his shirt but a great deal more would be wasted than the horse would be able to suck into his system, and there was no way of knowing how long it might be before there'd be any chance of replenishing their supply. Some quirk of Burt's nature put it into his head that if the horse couldn't drink why then he wouldn't drink either. He owed a hell of a lot to that gelding and he wasn't the kind of a guy to forget it.

Near noon he shot a bobcat and cooked a slab of the gamey meat over a slow fire and ate it more from a sense of need than for any pleasure it gave his palate. During this interval he slipped off the horse's bridle and let the animal graze.

At close to three they were pretty well into the foothills and, shortly after four, they found water; beside this spring they made camp and spent the night. Burt was still uneasy in his mind about Stiles and none too confident about Chacon either.

This whole deal, of course, was near as much in Stiles' favor as it was to Burt's own. Billy had said that he had also been promised to be let off lightly and the prospect of pocketing all the bounty on Chacon had ought to be enough to keep him reasonably honest. It was actually Chacon Burt supposed he should be worried about; and, so far as that went, he was worried about him. Because the lure of Greene's horses didn't someway seem enough to fetch the Mexican into a cooked-up contact with a pair of *gringos* he'd no reason to trust, not to say a word about the wholly unknown and supposed jail-breaker who was to provide the final details on the where and the how of taking over those horses.

Burt *himself* could be the bait which was fetching Chacon into this, the bandit's desire to get Burt under his thumb again. Who could say for sure what went on behind those whiskers— what greeds or black impulse would bring the man out from cover?

Or—and the thought came to him with a suddenness that made his guts turn cold and crawl—maybe Chacon had never been figured to appear in this deal. Maybe that Ranger was playing Burt for a sucker and the details hatched out between Mossman and Stiles had no further object than to put Burt Alvord behind the steel bars of Yuma!

TWENTY-ONE

Paludo

The north side of San Jose Mountain, Stiles had said, was where Burt could look for the Mexican to meet him; all four of them after that would get together at Carizzo Springs.

The peculiarity of this arrangement had not at once occurred to Alvord. His unhealed wrist had been giving him a great deal of pain and a lot of his thinking had been tied up with Bella and his hopes for the hereafter so that most of his worrying about Stiles had hinged on the man's repeated insistence that he meet Chacon alone.

As he neared the outskirts of Greene's holdings about the town of Cananea, however, this aspect of Stiles' instructions began more forcibly to engage Burt's interest. Carizzo Springs was some twenty-five miles south of the Mexican border town of Naco whereas San Jose Mountain lay between the two and a considerable distance nearer to the international fence. Mossman's stated desire was to lay hands on Chacon just as close to that fence as possible, so why had Stiles selected the springs for their rendezvous instead of the much handier mountain camp at which Burt was to meet the man they were after?

245

The more he considered this the more Burt was inclined to trust the good faith of Mossman. Chacon was dangerous as a skin-shedding rattler but, like the old saying had it, you never had to wonder what your enemies would do. Even a fool would keep his eyes peeled around a jasper like Paludo, but it was Stiles who had made the arrangements.

On a sudden inexplicable impulse Burt rode into Cananea and bought himself a straw sombrero, a cheap *zarape* and a .41 derringer in a .45 frame, single action. This was called among gamblers a "stingy gun" and had a very short barrel which was handy for close work. The hat he needed to protect his bald head. The heavy Mexican blanket he thought would make him less conspicuous in a region where two out of every three men generally packed one. The pistol he bought almost purely on hunch, a vague kind of feeling that it might come in handy to have an ace in the hole. He bought a little wooden box of cartridges to go with it and felt a little less like the frazzled end of a misspent life when he stepped out of the store and climbed back into his saddle. He was reasonably sure he had not been recognized and, darkly bronzed by the sun, in this hat and *zarape* and with his command of the language he could pass for a Mexican without keeping his mind on it. The pistol, loaded, he dropped into his right boot.

It was not so much an act of affection as just plain good business which caused him to stop at a livery stable just before he put the fringes of Cananea behind him. Those rocks they'd been through coming over the mountains had played hell with the gelding's shoes; they were paper-thin by this time and one of them was just about ready to drop off. He had the horse reshod, afterwards standing him to a good feed of oats and taking behind his cantle an additional twenty-five pound sack of the same for the animal's future enjoyment.

It was dark when he quit the livery and this was exactly the way Burt wanted it. Instead of taking the trail northeast toward his objective, he left Greene's town on the road to Bacoachic and stayed with it for ten miles before swinging east through the hills to find a campsite for the night. It was ten-fifteen when he unsaddled beside a creek in the shelter of tall pines and turned the gelding loose on hobbles. He rested him there on grain and good grass until about four o'clock of the next afternoon, at which time he resaddled and set out for San Jose Mountain which he could see in the northern distance.

This was the tenth day out from Minas Prietas, the day on which—according to Stiles—he was due to meet up with Augustin Chacon. Burt figured it might be smart not to follow Stiles' instructions too carefully. If the Mexican was already waiting it wouldn't hurt him a bit to cool his heels awhile longer and Burt hadn't the slightest intention of spending more time in his company than necessary. The rendezvous with Stiles and Mossman had been set for the following morning and all the Ranger had asked Burt to do was to put him in touch with Chacon somewhere close to the Arizona border.

This was what Burt had in mind. Carizzo Springs was a considerable distance from the border and Burt wasn't aiming to go anyplace near it. If Stiles' strategy, whatever it was, depended on contacting Alvord and Chacon in that particular vicinity he had better get about shaping up some other strategy.

Burt spent the night on the east flank of the mountain, going up there after dark. When the first flush of daylight broke over the tumbled slopes he was hunkered on his bootheels about a hundred yards above the place where Chacon was supposed to be meeting him. He could see no sign of the outlaw's presence and there was no smell of woodsmoke.

But, just as he was about to go down to investigate, he caught from the grove of spruce at his right the sudden thump of a hobbled horse. Almost at once his glance picked out the peaked hat of Paludo.

The man was crouched much as Burt had been

with his back to the slope, silently watching the camp. There was a buffalo gun lying ready across his lap. Burt considered slipping down and trying to get the drop on him, but gave it up as being too dangerous; Mossman hadn't asked Burt to deliver Chacon hogtied, so why take the risk?

An hour dragged past punctuated by bird songs and the occasional thump of the bandit's hobbled horse. Burt had left his own horse around the shoulder of the mountain.

Chacon presently got up, stretched the cramps from his body and seemed about to head down toward the camp when Alvord called him.

Chacon spun like a flash.

"*Buenas dias*," Alvord grinned, and the bandit's whiskered features turned ludicrous when he observed Burt lounging above him with a thumb casually hooked in the sag of crossed gun belts.

"What you do up there?"

"Waitin' for you to go down an' fix breakfast. What were you doing?"

"I been watch for you, *amigo*—for why you no come other day?"

Alvord shrugged. "We got plenty of time. There's a bottle of *tequila* for you on my saddle; throw some grub on the fire while I go fetch it."

He turned away without waiting for the Mexican's assent, though the flesh on his back did considerable writhing in expectation of a bullet till he got beyond accurate range of

Chacon's carbine. The man was obviously in one of his uglier moods so, after Burt swung into the saddle, he rode a wide circle which brought him into the camp from an unexpected angle.

Chacon had fetched in his horse and got a smokeless fire going and the delectable odor of *frijoles y chile* made Burt smack his lips as he ground-hitched the gelding in a patch of blue shadow where the seep from a spring made the grass green and tall.

He dropped the bottle near the outlaw and hunkered down across the fire from him, scooping some of the beans into a soft flour *tortilla* and washing the mixture down with great gulps of strong black java. Chacon had made no move to touch the bottle and all the time they were eating Alvord tried to engage him in aimless conversation but the most he got was a couple of sour grunts. Not once did Chacon remove the weight of his glance and at last it began to get on Burt's nerves.

"If you don't want the horses then for Chri—"

"What horses?" A suggestion of surprise ran through the bandit's surly stare and Alvord went cold clean down to his bootsoles. It was more than enough to confirm all his suspicions, but he tried to carry it off, saying lightly, "It was a horse-liftin' spree I was figurin' to take you on, but if—"

"I think you lie, *gringo*!"

Alvord sucked in his breath.

Paludo's eyes rolled out a wildness bright and wicked as summer lightning. Conviction hammered the piano-wire tautness of all Burt's gathered faculties as he suddenly glimpsed the probable path of Stiles' greed-spawned duplicity.

The man had baited his trap with something surer than horses!

Alvord cursed himself for not guessing it sooner.

Nothing but the prospect of blood could have whetted this butcher to such a pitch of excitement as now glared out of his white-rimmed stare.

The stung pride of Stiles' failure to uncover Burt's loot had shown the way to both revenge and profit; by playing the Judas role once more he had placed Burt Alvord where Chacon could kill him. Armed then with his body Stiles could trek back to Tombstone and claim the law's bounty while Chacon held Mossman for ransom!

The loneliness of this mountainside closed in upon Alvord like the walls of a cage. His incredible speed with a gun could not help him while Paludo was fingering the trigger of that carbine. At the first sign of danger flame would leap out of it to send whining death crashing into Burt's guts.

And then—slim chance—Alvord's mind recalled something.

He forced a parched grin. "Why would I lie to an old friend like you?" He made his eyes smile into the blaze of Chacon's black ones. How long would his talk hold the squeeze off that trigger?

He passed his dry tongue across the rasp of drier lips. "What did Stiles—*Christ!*" he shouted on an outrush of breath, and sent his jackknifing body slamming sideways. The groan wrenched out of his twisted mouth was not for the crash of Paludo's carbine, whose slug missed his head by screaming inches, but for the weight thrown onto that unhealed wrist. Before Chacon could jack another cartridge into the breach Alvord had the derringer out of his boot and its snout rammed hard against the Mexican's middle. "One squeak, by God, an' you're for hell on a shutter!"

The man was mightily tempted—you could see it in the blaze of those berserk eyes. But he hadn't the mental equipment to act fast enough. By the time he realized the gun was gone from his belly its barrel was whacking him across the left temple. He sprawled onto his face like a sack of wet wash.

Alvord jerked Chacon's pistol, pulled the man's thick wrists behind his back and grimly lashed them. Then he knocked the neck off the untouched bottle and poured a good half of the stuff down his throat.

It was just what the doctor ordered.

• • •

Alvord left Chacon tied for the rest of the day.

He wasn't worried about Mossman going off without finding him. Obviously Stiles, when he'd mapped this job out with the Mexican, had never intended they should meet at Carizzo Springs; that was dust thrown to blind his friend Alvord and the Ranger. Whenever Cap Mossman got disgusted with waiting Stiles would suggest they take a look around up here. If Mossman displayed any reasonable caution Stiles wouldn't start anything before Chacon's proximity could make results doubly certain. So Burt reckoned if he waited long enough they'd show up here.

And, sure enough, they did.

It was along about five in the afternoon when his watching glance picked them out of the brush some three miles below the start of the trail. He made some snap calculations and arrived at the notion they'd hit camp around eight if left to their own devices. Then he reckoned it might be a shade more amusing if Chacon and himself should meet up with them somewhat sooner.

Going over to the trussed-up and glowering *bandido*, he unbuckled the man's shell belt and, taking it off to one side but where Paludo would be able to observe what was happening, got to work with his knife on the cartridges it held. One by one he removed their slugs, dumped out the powder and tamped the now harmless bullets back in again. He threw Chacon's knife forty feet into a manzanita thicket and then took care of the loads in Chacon's pistol, afterwards sliding the gun into its sheath and rebuckling the belt about the killer's waist.

"*Salud!*" he said, grinning. "Pretty soon, *mi amigo*, you'll be ready to make tracks—only this time they ain't goin' to be snake ones."

He picked up Chacon's carbine and with a rock broke off both the hammer and trigger before thrusting the weapon into the scabbard on Paludo's saddle. He readied both horses and cut Chacon loose.

"There's your bronc—climb on him. Just remember one thing, my long-whiskered *compadre*. I'm a damned good shot so take off any time you've a mind to."

It was shortly after nine and without much light save what filtered from the stars when Alvord spotted a pair of horsemen climbing toward them. Stiles called out a cautious greeting and Burt laughed with real relish at the stiffness which suddenly came over the gunman when he saw how his plans had miscarried. "Fine night," he said, chuckling, and greeted the Ranger as *amigo*. Then he beckoned Cap aside.

"The deal," he said, "as I understood it was for me to fetch you Chacon somewheres close to the border. You satisfied I've done it?"

Mossman nodded. "But you've still got to give yourself up if we're to help you."

"I'll do the right thing, you can count on that. An' you needn't worry about Chacon; I've dumped all his powder. Just keep your eye on Billy Stiles an' you won't have any trouble."

"You pulling out now?"

"Damned right," Alvord grunted. "Where'd you say I'd find Bella?"

Center Point Large Print
600 Brooks Road / PO Box 1
Thorndike, ME 04986-0001 USA

(207) 568-3717

US & Canada:
1 800 929-9108
www.centerpointlargeprint.com